WILL YOU PLEASE BE QUIET, PLEASE?

Raymond Carver was born in Clatskanie, Oregon in 1938. He married early and for years his writing had to come second to earning a living for his young family. Despite some early publication by small presses, it was not until the success of *Will You Please Be Quiet, Please?* that his work began to reach a larger audience. This was the year that he gave up alcohol, and in 1977, after the break-up of his marriage, he met the writer Tess Gallagher with whom he spent the last eleven years of his life. During this prolific period he wrote three collections of stories, *What We Talk About When We Talk About Love*, *Cathedral* and *Elephant*. *Fires*, a book of essays, poems and stories appeared in 1985, and in 1987 he published *In a Marine Light*, a volume of selected poems. He completed his last book of poems, *A New Path to the Waterfall*, shortly before his death in 1988.

ALSO BY RAYMOND CARVER

Fiction

Furious Seasons

What We Talk About When We Talk About Love

Cathedral

Elephant

Where I'm Calling From: The Selected Stories
(with the author's foreword)

Short Cuts
(selected and with an introduction by Robert Altman)

Call Me if You Need Me: The Uncollected Fiction & Prose
(edited by William L. Stull with a foreword by
Tess Gallagher)

Poetry

Near Klamath

Winter Insomnia

At Night the Salmon Move

Where Water Comes Together with Other Water

Ultramarine

In a Marine Light: Selected Poems

A New Path to the Waterfall
(with an introduction by Tess Gallagher)

All of Us: The Collected Poems
(edited by William L. Stull)

Essays, Poems, Stories

Fires

No Heroics, Please

Raymond Carver

WILL YOU PLEASE BE QUIET, PLEASE?

VINTAGE BOOKS
London

THIS BOOK IS FOR MARYANN

Published by Vintage 2003

8 10 9

First published in the USA in 1976 by
McGraw-Hill

First published in Great Britain in 1995
in a revised single volume edition by
The Harvill Press

Vintage
Random House, 20 Vauxhall Bridge Road,
London SW1V 2SA

www.vintage-books.co.uk

Addresses for companies within The Random House Group Limited
can be found at: www.randomhouse.co.uk/offices.htm

The Random House Group Limited Reg. No. 954009

A CIP catalogue record for this book
is available from the British Library

ISBN 9780099449898

The Random House Group Limited supports The Forest Stewardship
Council (FSC), the leading international forest certification
organisation. All our titles that are printed on Greenpeace approved
FSC certified paper carry the FSC logo. Our paper procurement
policy can be found at: www.rbooks.co.uk/environment

Printed in the UK by CPI Bookmarque Ltd, Croydon, CR0 4TD

CONTENTS

A NOTE ON THE TEXT

The stories in this collection are arranged in the order in which they appeared in the first edition published by McGraw-Hill, New York, 1976. The following stories were revised by the author for *Where I'm Calling from: The Selected Stories*: (Atlantic Monthly Press, New York, 1988 and Harvill, London, 1993) and in one case the title was changed: "Fat", "Neighbors", "They're Not Your Husband" "Nobody Said Anything", "What's in Alaska?", "Collectors", "What Do You Do in San Francisco?", "The Student's Wife", "Put Yourself in My Shoes", "Why, Honey?", "Bicycles, Muscles, Cigarettes", "Are These Actual Miles?" (originally "What Is It?").

WILL YOU PLEASE
BE QUIET, PLEASE?

Fat

I am sitting over coffee and cigarettes at my friend Rita's and I am telling her about it.

Here is what I tell her.

It is late of a slow Wednesday when Herb seats the fat man at my station.

This fat man is the fattest person I have ever seen, though he is neat-appearing and well dressed enough. Everything about him is big. But it is the fingers I remember best. When I stop at the table near his to see to the old couple, I first notice the fingers. They look three times the size of a normal person's fingers – long, thick, creamy fingers.

I see to my other tables, a party of four businessmen, very demanding, another party of four, three men and a woman, and this old couple. Leander has poured the fat man's water, and I give the fat man plenty of time to make up his mind before going over.

Good evening, I say. May I serve you? I say.

Rita, he was big, I mean big.

Good evening, he says. Hello. Yes, he says. I think we're ready to order now, he says.

He has this way of speaking – strange, don't you know. And he makes a little puffing sound every so often.

I think we will begin with a Caesar salad, he says. And then a bowl of soup with some extra bread and butter, if you please. The lamb chops, I believe, he says. And baked potato with sour cream. We'll see about dessert later. Thank you very much, he says, and hands me the menu.

God, Rita, but those were fingers.

I hurry away to the kitchen and turn in the order to Rudy, who takes it with a face. You know Rudy. Rudy is that way when he works.

As I come out of the kitchen, Margo – I've told you about Margo? The one who chases Rudy? Margo says to me, Who's your fat friend? He's really a fatty.

* * *

Now that's part of it. I think that is really part of it.

I make the Caesar salad there at his table, him watching my every move, meanwhile buttering pieces of bread and laying them off to one side, all the time making this puffing noise. Anyway, I am so keyed up or something, I knock over his glass of water.

I'm so sorry, I say. It always happens when you get into a hurry. I'm very sorry, I say. Are you all right? I'll get the boy to clean up right away, I say.

It's nothing, he says. It's all right, he says, and he puffs. Don't worry about it, we don't mind, he says. He smiles and waves as I go off to get Leander, and when I come back to serve the salad, I see the fat man has eaten all his bread and butter.

A little later, when I bring him more bread, he has finished his salad. You know the size of those Caesar salads?

You're very kind, he says. This bread is marvelous, he says.

Thank you, I say.

Well, it is very good, he says, and we mean that. We don't often enjoy bread like this, he says.

Where are you from? I ask him. I don't believe I've seen you before, I say.

He's not the kind of person you'd forget, Rita puts in with a snicker.

Denver, he says.

I don't say anything more on the subject, though I am curious.

Your soup will be along in a few minutes, sir, I say, and I go off to put the finishing touches to my party of four businessmen, very demanding.

When I serve his soup, I see the bread has disappeared again. He is just putting the last piece of bread into his mouth.

Believe me, he says, we don't eat like this all the time, he says. And puffs. You'll have to excuse us, he says.

Don't think a thing about it, please, I say. I like to see a man eat and enjoy himself, I say.

I don't know, he says. I guess that's what you'd call it. And puffs. He arranges the napkin. Then he picks up his spoon.

God, he's fat! says Leander.

He can't help it, I say, so shut up.

I put down another basket of bread and more butter. How was the soup? I say.

Thank you. Good, he says. Very good, he says. He wipes his lips and dabs his chin. Do you think it's warm in here, or is it just me? he says.

No, it is warm in here, I say.

Maybe we'll take off our coat, he says.

Go right ahead, I say. A person has to be comfortable, I say.

That's true, he says, that is very, very true, he says.

But I see a little later that he is still wearing his coat.

My large parties are gone now and also the old couple. The place is emptying out. By the time I serve the fat man his chops and baked potato, along with more bread and butter, he is the only one left.

I drop lots of sour cream onto his potato. I sprinkle bacon and chives over his sour cream. I bring him more bread and butter.

Is everything all right? I say.

Fine, he says, and he puffs. Excellent, thank you, he says, and puffs again.

Enjoy your dinner, I say. I raise the lid of his sugar bowl and look in. He nods and keeps looking at me until I move away.

I know now I was after something. But I don't know what.

How is old tub-of-guts doing? He's going to run your legs off, says Harriet. You know Harriet.

For dessert, I say to the fat man, there is the Green Lantern Special, which is a pudding cake with sauce, or there is cheesecake or vanilla ice cream or pineapple sherbet.

We're not making you late, are we? he says, puffing and looking concerned.

Not at all, I say. Of course not, I say. Take your time, I say. I'll bring you more coffee while you make up your mind.

We'll be honest with you, he says. And he moves in the seat. We would like the Special, but we may have a dish of vanilla ice cream as well. With just a drop of chocolate syrup, if you please. We told you we were hungry, he says.

I go off to the kitchen to see after his dessert myself, and Rudy says, Harriet says you got a fat man from the circus out there. That true?

Rudy has his apron and hat off now, if you see what I mean.

Rudy, he is fat, I say, but that is not the whole story.

Rudy just laughs.

Sounds to me like she's sweet on fat-stuff, he says.

Better watch out, Rudy, says Joanne, who just that minute comes into the kitchen.

I'm getting jealous, Rudy says to Joanne.

I put the Special in front of the fat man and a big bowl of vanilla ice cream with chocolate syrup to the side.

Thank you, he says.

You are very welcome, I say – and a feeling comes over me.

Believe it or not, he says, we have not always eaten like this.

Me, I eat and I eat and I can't gain, I say. I'd like to gain, I say.

No, he says. If we had our choice, no. But there is no choice.

Then he picks up his spoon and eats.

What else? Rita says, lighting one of my cigarettes and pulling her chair closer to the table. This story's getting interesting now, Rita says.

That's it. Nothing else. He eats his desserts, and then he leaves and then we go home, Rudy and me.

Some fatty, Rudy says, stretching like he does when he's tired. Then he just laughs and goes back to watching the TV.

I put the water on to boil for tea and take a shower. I put my hand on my middle and wonder what would happen if I had children and one of them turned out to look like that, so fat.

I pour the water in the pot, arrange the cups, the sugar bowl, carton of half and half, and take the tray in to Rudy. As if he's been thinking about it, Rudy says, I knew a fat guy once, a couple of fat guys, really fat guys, when I was a kid. They were tubbies, my God. I don't remember their names. Fat, that's the only name this one kid had. We called him Fat, the kid who lived next door to me. He was a neighbor. The other kid came along later. His name was Wobbly. Everybody called him Wobbly except the teachers. Wobbly and Fat. Wish I had their pictures, Rudy says.

I can't think of anything to say, so we drink our tea and pretty soon I get up to go to bed. Rudy gets up too, turns off the TV, locks the front door, and begins his unbuttoning.

I get into bed and move clear over to the edge and lie there on my stomach. But right away, as soon as he turns off the light and gets into bed, Rudy begins. I turn on my back and relax some, though it is against my will. But here is the thing. When he gets on me, I suddenly feel I am fat. I feel I am terrifically fat, so fat that Rudy is a tiny thing and hardly there at all.

That's a funny story, Rita says, but I can see she doesn't know what to make of it.

I feel depressed. But I won't go into it with her. I've already told her too much.

She sits there waiting, her dainty fingers poking her hair.

Waiting for what? I'd like to know.

It is August.

My life is going to change. I feel it.

Neighbors

Bill and Arlene Miller were a happy couple. But now and then they felt they alone among their circle had been passed by somehow, leaving Bill to attend to his bookkeeping duties and Arlene occupied with secretarial chores. They talked about it sometimes, mostly in comparison with the lives of their neighbors, Harriet and Jim Stone. It seemed to the Millers that the Stones lived a fuller and brighter life. The Stones were always going out for dinner, or entertaining at home, or traveling about the country somewhere in connection with Jim's work.

The Stones lived across the hall from the Millers. Jim was a salesman for a machine-parts firm and often managed to combine business with pleasure trips, and on this occasion the Stones would be away for ten days, first to Cheyenne, then on to St Louis to visit relatives. In their absence, the Millers would look after the Stones' apartment, feed Kitty, and water the plants.

Bill and Jim shook hands beside the car. Harriet and Arlene held each other by the elbows and kissed lightly on the lips.

"Have fun," Bill said to Harriet.

"We will," said Harriet. "You kids have fun too."

Arlene nodded.

Jim winked at her. "Bye, Arlene. Take good care of the old man."

"I will," Arlene said.

"Have fun," Bill said.

"You bet," Jim said, clipping Bill lightly on the arm. "And thanks again, you guys."

The Stones waved as they drove away, and the Millers waved too.

"Well, I wish it was us," Bill said.

"God knows, we could use a vacation," Arlene said. She took his arm and put it around her waist as they climbed the stairs to their apartment.

After dinner Arlene said, "Don't forget. Kitty gets liver flavor the first night." She stood in the kitchen doorway folding the handmade tablecloth that Harriet had bought for her last year in Santa Fe.

Bill took a deep breath as he entered the Stones' apartment. The air was already heavy and it was vaguely sweet. The sunburst clock over the television said half past eight. He remembered when Harriet had come home with the clock, how she had crossed the hall to show it to Arlene, cradling the brass case in her arms and talking to it through the tissue paper as if it were an infant.

Kitty rubbed her face against his slippers and then turned onto her side, but jumped up quickly as Bill moved to the kitchen and selected one of the stacked cans from the gleaming drainboard. Leaving the cat to pick at her food, he headed for the bathroom. He looked at himself in the mirror and then closed his eyes and then looked again. He opened the medicine chest. He found a container of pills and read the label – *Harriet Stone. One each day as directed* – and slipped it into his pocket. He went back to the kitchen, drew a pitcher of water, and returned to the living room. He finished watering, set the pitcher on the rug, and opened the liquor cabinet. He reached in back for the bottle of Chivas Regal. He took two drinks from the bottle, wiped his lips on his sleeve, and replaced the bottle in the cabinet.

Kitty was on the couch sleeping. He switched off the lights, slowly closing and checking the door. He had the feeling he had left something.

"What kept you?" Arlene said. She sat with her legs turned under her, watching television.

"Nothing. Playing with Kitty," he said, and went over to her and touched her breasts.

"Let's go to bed, honey," he said.

The next day Bill took only ten minutes of the twenty-minute break allotted for the afternoon and left at fifteen minutes before five. He parked the car in the lot just as Arlene hopped down from the bus. He waited until she entered the building, then ran up the stairs to catch her as she stepped out of the elevator.

"Bill! God, you scared me. You're early," she said.

He shrugged. "Nothing to do at work," he said.

She let him use her key to open the door. He looked at the door

7

across the hall before following her inside.

"Let's go to bed," he said.

"Now?" She laughed. "What's gotten into you?"

"Nothing. Take your dress off." He grabbed for her awkwardly, and she said, "Good God, Bill."

He unfastened his belt.

Later they sent out for Chinese food, and when it arrived they ate hungrily, without speaking, and listened to records.

"Let's not forget to feed Kitty," she said.

"I was just thinking about that," he said. "I'll go right over."

He selected a can of fish flavor for the cat, then filled the pitcher and went to water. When he returned to the kitchen, the cat was scratching in her box. She looked at him steadily before she turned back to the litter. He opened all the cupboards and examined the canned goods, the cereals, the packaged foods, the cocktail and wine glasses, the china, the pots and pans. He opened the refrigerator. He sniffed some celery, took two bites of cheddar cheese, and chewed on an apple as he walked into the bedroom. The bed seemed enormous, with a fluffy white bedspread draped to the floor. He pulled out a nightstand drawer, found a half-empty package of cigarettes and stuffed them into his pocket. Then he stepped to the closet and was opening it when the knock sounded at the front door.

He stopped by the bathroom and flushed the toilet on his way.

"What's been keeping you?" Arlene said. "You've been over here more than an hour."

"Have I really?" he said.

"Yes, you have," she said.

"I had to go to the toilet," he said.

"You have your own toilet," she said.

"I couldn't wait," he said.

That night they made love again.

In the morning he had Arlene call in for him. He showered, dressed, and made a light breakfast. He tried to start a book. He went out for a walk and felt better. But after a while, hands still in his pockets, he returned to the apartment. He stopped at the Stones' door on the chance he might hear the cat moving about. Then he let himself in at his own door and went to the kitchen for the key.

Inside it seemed cooler than his apartment, and darker too. He wondered if the plants had something to do with the temperature of the air. He looked out the window, and then he moved slowly through each room considering everything that fell under his gaze, carefully, one object at a time. He saw ashtrays, items of furniture, kitchen utensils, the clock. He saw everything. At last he entered the bedroom, and the cat appeared at his feet. He stroked her once, carried her into the bathroom, and shut the door.

He lay down on the bed and stared at the ceiling. He lay for a while with his eyes closed, and then he moved his hand under his belt. He tried to recall what day it was. He tried to remember when the Stones were due back, and then he wondered if they would ever return. He could not remember their faces or the way they talked and dressed. He sighed and with effort rolled off the bed to lean over the dresser and look at himself in the mirror.

He opened the closet and selected a Hawaiian shirt. He looked until he found Bermudas, neatly pressed and hanging over a pair of brown twill slacks. He shed his own clothes and slipped into the shorts and the shirt. He looked in the mirror again. He went to the living room and poured himself a drink and sipped it on his way back to the bedroom. He put on a blue shirt, a dark suit, a blue and white tie, black wing-tip shoes. The glass was empty and he went for another drink.

In the bedroom again, he sat on a chair, crossed his legs, and smiled, observing himself in the mirror. The telephone rang twice and fell silent. He finished the drink and took off the suit. He rummaged through the top drawers until he found a pair of panties and a brassiere. He stepped into the panties and fastened the brassiere, then looked through the closet for an outfit. He put on a black and white checkered skirt and tried to zip it up. He put on a burgundy blouse that buttoned up the front. He considered her shoes, but understood they would not fit. For a long time he looked out the living-room window from behind the curtain. Then he returned to the bedroom and put everything away.

He was not hungry. She did not eat much, either. They looked at each other shyly and smiled. She got up from the table and checked that the key was on the shelf and then she quickly cleared the dishes.

He stood in the kitchen doorway and smoked a cigarette and watched her pick up the key.

"Make yourself comfortable while I go across the hall," she said. "Read the paper or something." She closed her fingers over the key. He was, she said, looking tired.

He tried to concentrate on the news. He read the paper and turned on the television. Finally he went across the hall. The door was locked.

"It's me. Are you still there, honey?" he called.

After a time the lock released and Arlene stepped outside and shut the door. "Was I gone so long?" she said.

"Well, you were," he said.

"Was I?" she said. "I guess I must have been playing with Kitty."

He studied her, and she looked away, her hand still resting on the doorknob.

"It's funny," she said. "You know – to go in someone's place like that."

He nodded, took her hand from the knob, and guided her toward their own door. He let them into their apartment.

"It *is* funny," he said.

He noticed white lint clinging to the back of her sweater, and the color was high in her cheeks. He began kissing her on the neck and hair and she turned and kissed him back.

"Oh, damn," she said. "Damn, damn," she sang, girlishly clapping her hands. "I just remembered. I really and truly forgot to do what I went over there to do. I didn't feed Kitty or do any watering." She looked at him. "Isn't that stupid?"

"I don't think so," he said. "Just a minute. I'll get my cigarettes and go back with you."

She waited until he had closed and locked their door, and then she took his arm at the muscle and said. "I guess I should tell you. I found some pictures."

He stopped in the middle of the hall. "What kind of pictures?"

"You can see for yourself," she said, and she watched him.

"No kidding." He grinned. "Where?"

"In a drawer," she said.

"No kidding," he said.

And then she said, "Maybe they won't come back," and was at once astonished at her words.

"It could happen," he said. "Anything could happen."

"Or maybe they'll come back and . . ." but she did not finish.

They held hands for the short walk across the hall, and when he spoke she could barely hear his voice.

"The key," he said. "Give it to me."

"What?" she said. She gazed at the door.

"The key," he said. "You have the key."

"My God," she said, "I left the key inside."

He tried the knob. It was locked. Then she tried the knob. It would not turn. Her lips were parted, and her breathing was hard, expectant. He opened his arms and she moved into them.

"Don't worry," he said into her ear. "For God's sake, don't worry."

They stayed there. They held each other. They leaned into the door as if against a wind, and braced themselves.

The Idea

We'd finished supper and I'd been at the kitchen table with the light out for the last hour, watching. If he was going to do it tonight, it was time, past time. I hadn't seen him in three nights. But tonight the bedroom shade was up over there and the light burning.

I had a feeling tonight.

Then I saw him. He opened the screen and walked out onto his back porch wearing a T-shirt and something like Bermuda shorts or a swimsuit. He looked around once and hopped off the porch into the shadows and began to move along the side of the house. He was fast. If I hadn't been watching, I wouldn't have seen him. He stopped in front of the lighted window and looked in.

"Vern," I called. "Vern, hurry up! He's out there. You'd better hurry!"

Vern was in the living room reading his paper with the TV going. I heard him throw down the paper.

"Don't let him see you!" Vern said. "Don't get up too close to the window!"

Vern always says that: Don't get up too close. Vern's a little embarrassed about watching, I think. But I know he enjoys it. He's said so.

"He can't see us with the light out." It's what I always say. This has been going on for three months. Since September 3, to be exact. Anyway, that's the first night I saw him over there. I don't know how long it was going on before that.

I almost got on the phone to the sheriff that night, until I recognized who it was out there. It took Vern to explain it to me. Even then it took a while for it to penetrate. But since that night I've watched, and I can tell you he averages one out of every two or three nights, sometimes more. I've seen him out there when it's been raining too. In fact, if it *is* raining, you can bet on seeing him. But tonight it was clear and windy. There was a moon.

We got down on our knees behind the window and Vern cleared his throat.

"Look at him," Vern said. Vern was smoking, knocking the ash into his hand when he needed. He held the cigarette away from the window when he puffed. Vern smokes all the time; there's no stopping him. He even sleeps with an ashtray three inches from his head. At night I'm awake and he wakes up and smokes.

"By God," Vern said.

"What does she have that other women don't have?" I said to Vern after a minute. We were hunkered on the floor with just our heads showing over the windowsill and were looking at a man who was standing and looking into his own bedroom window.

"That's just it," Vern said. He cleared his throat right next to my ear. We kept watching.

I could make out someone behind the curtain now. It must have been her undressing. But I couldn't see any detail. I strained my eyes. Vern was wearing his reading glasses, so he could see everything better than I could. Suddenly the curtain was drawn aside and the woman turned her back to the window.

"What's she doing now?" I said, knowing full well.

"By God," Vern said.

"What's she doing, Vern?" I said.

"She's taking off her clothes," Vern said. "What do you think she's doing?"

Then the bedroom light went out and the man started back along the side of his house. He opened the screen door and slipped inside, and a little later the rest of the lights went out.

Vern coughed, coughed again, and shook his head. I turned on the light. Vern just sat there on his knees. Then he got to his feet and lighted a cigarette.

"Someday I'm going to tell that trash what I think of her," I said and looked at Vern.

Vern laughed sort of.

"I mean it," I said. "I'll see her in the market someday and I'll tell her to her face."

"I wouldn't do that. What the hell would you do that for?" Vern said.

But I could tell he didn't think I was serious. He frowned and looked at his nails. He rolled his tongue in his mouth and narrowed his eyes like he does when he's concentrating. Then his expression changed and he scratched his chin. "You wouldn't do anything like that," he said.

"You'll see," I said.

"Shit," Vern said.

I followed him into the living room. We were jumpy. It gets us like that.

"You wait," I said.

Vern ground his cigarette out in the big ashtray. He stood beside his leather chair and looked at the TV a minute.

"There's never anything on," he said. Then he said something else. He said, "Maybe he *has* something there." Vern lighted another cigarette. "You don't know."

"Anybody comes looking in my window," I said, "they'll have the cops on them. Except maybe Cary Grant," I said.

Vern shrugged. "You don't know," he said.

I had an appetite. I went to the kitchen cupboard and looked, and then I opened the fridge.

"Vern, you want something to eat?" I called.

He didn't answer. I could hear water running in the bathroom. But I thought he might want something. We get hungry this time of night. I put bread and lunchmeat on the table and I opened a can of soup. I got out crackers and peanut butter, cold meat loaf, pickles, olives, potato chips. I put everything on the table. Then I thought of the apple pie.

Vern came out in his robe and flannel pajamas. His hair was wet and slicked down over the back of his head, and he smelled of toilet water. He looked at the things on the table. He said, "What about a bowl of corn flakes with brown sugar?" Then he sat down and spread his paper out to the side of his plate.

We ate our snack. The ashtray filled up with olive pits and his butts. When he'd finished, Vern grinned and said, "What's that good smell?"

I went to the oven and took out the two pieces of apple pie topped with melted cheese.

"That looks fine," Vern said.

In a little while, he said. "I can't eat any more. I'm going to bed."

"I'm coming too," I said. "I'll clear this table."

I was scraping plates into the garbage can when I saw the ants. I looked closer. They came from somewhere beneath the pipes under the sink, a steady stream of them, up one side of the can and down the other, coming and going. I found the spray in one of the drawers and sprayed the outside and the inside of the garbage can, and I sprayed as far back under the sink as I could reach. Then I washed my hands and took a last look around the kitchen.

Vern was asleep. He was snoring. He'd wake up in a few hours, go to the bathroom, and smoke. The little TV at the foot of the bed was on, but the picture was rolling.

I'd wanted to tell Vern about the ants.

I took my own time getting ready for bed, fixed the picture, and crawled in. Vern made the noises he does in his sleep.

I watched for a while, but it was a talk show and I don't like talk shows. I started thinking about the ants again.

Pretty soon I imagined them all over the house. I wondered if I should wake Vern and tell him I was having a bad dream. Instead, I got up and went for the can of spray. I looked under the sink again. But there was no ants left. I turned on every light in the house until I had the house blazing.

I kept spraying.

Finally I raised the shade in the kitchen and looked out. It was late. The wind blew and I heard branches snap.

"That trash," I said. "The idea!"

I used even worse language, things I can't repeat.

They're Not Your Husband

Earl Ober was between jobs as a salesman. But Doreen, his wife, had gone to work nights as a waitress at a twenty-four-hour coffee shop at the edge of town. One night, when he was drinking, Earl decided to stop by the coffee shop and have something to eat. He wanted to see where Doreen worked, and he wanted to see if he could order something on the house.

He sat at the counter and studied the menu.

"What are you doing here?" Doreen said when she saw him sitting there.

She handed over an order to the cook. "What are you going to order, Earl?" she said. "The kids okay?"

"They're fine," Earl said. "I'll have coffee and one of those Number Two sandwiches."

Doreen wrote it down.

"Any chance of, you know?" he said to her and winked.

"No," she said. "Don't talk to me now. I'm busy."

Earl drank his coffee and waited for the sandwich. Two men in business suits, their ties undone, their collars open, sat down next to him and asked for coffee. As Doreen walked away with the coffeepot, one of the men said to the other, "Look at the ass on that. I don't believe it."

The other man laughed. "I've seen better," he said.

"That's what I mean," the first man said. "But some jokers like their quim fat."

"Not me," the other man said.

"Not me, neither," the first man said. "That's what I was saying."

Doreen put the sandwich in front of Earl. Around the sandwich there were French fries, coleslaw, dill pickle.

"Anything else?" she said. "A glass of milk?"

He didn't say anything. He shook his head when she kept standing there.

"I'll get you more coffee," she said.

She came back with the pot and poured coffee for him and for the two men. Then she picked up a dish and turned to get some ice cream. She reached down into the container and with the dipper began to scoop up the ice cream. The white skirt yanked against her hips and crawled up her legs. What showed was girdle, and it was pink, thighs that were rumpled and gray and a little hairy, and veins that spread in a berserk display.

The two men sitting beside Earl exchanged looks. One of them raised his eyebrows. The other man grinned and kept looking at Doreen over his cup as she spooned chocolate syrup over the ice cream. When she began shaking the can of whipped cream, Earl got up, leaving his food, and headed for the door. He heard her call his name, but he kept going.

He checked on the children and then went to the other bedroom and took off his clothes. He pulled the covers up, closed his eyes, and allowed himself to think. The feeling started in his face and worked down into his stomach and legs. He opened his eyes and rolled his head back and forth on the pillow. Then he turned on his side and fell asleep.

In the morning, after she had sent the children off to school, Doreen came into the bedroom and raised the shade. Earl was already awake.

"Look at yourself in the mirror," he said.

"What?" she said. "What are you talking about?"

"Just look at yourself in the mirror," he said.

"What am I supposed to see?" she said. But she looked in the mirror over the dresser and pushed the hair away from her shoulders.

"Well?" he said.

"Well, what?" she said.

"I hate to say anything," Earl said, "but I think you better give a diet some thought. I mean it. I'm serious. I think you could lose a few pounds. Don't get mad."

"What are you saying?" she said.

"Just what I said. I think you could lose a few pounds. A few pounds, anyway," he said.

"You never said anything before," she said. She raised her nightgown over her hips and turned to look at her stomach in the mirror.

"I never felt it was a problem before," he said. He tried to pick his words.

The nightgown still gathered around her waist, Doreen turned her back to the mirror and looked over her shoulder. She raised one buttock in her hand and let it drop.

Earl closed his eyes. "Maybe I'm all wet," he said.

"I guess I could afford to lose. But it'd be hard," she said.

"You're right, it won't be easy," he said. "But I'll help."

"Maybe you're right," she said. She dropped her nightgown and looked at him and then she took her nightgown off.

They talked about diets. They talked about the protein diets, the vegetable-only diets, the grapefruit-juice diets. But they decided they didn't have the money to buy the steaks the protein diet called for. And Doreen said she didn't care for all that many vegetables. And since she didn't like grapefruit juice that much, she didn't see how she could do that one, either.

"Okay, forget it," he said.

"No, you're right," she said. "I'll do something."

"What about exercises?" he said.

"I'm getting all the exercise I need down there," she said.

"Just quit eating," Earl said. "For a few days, anyway."

"All right," she said. "I'll try. For a few days I'll give it a try. You've convinced me."

"I'm a closer," Earl said.

He figured up the balance in their checking account, then drove to the discount store and bought a bathroom scale. He looked the clerk over as she rang up the sale.

At home he had Doreen take off all her clothes and get on the scale. He frowned when he saw the veins. He ran his finger the length of one that sprouted up her thigh.

"What are you doing?" she asked.

"Nothing," he said.

He looked at the scale and wrote the figure down on a piece of paper.

"All right," Earl said. "All right."

The next day he was gone for most of the afternoon on an interview. The employer, a heavyset man who limped as he showed Earl around the plumbing fixtures in the warehouse, asked if Earl were free to travel.

"You bet I'm free," Earl said.

The man nodded.

Earl smiled.

* * *

He could hear the television before he opened the door to the house. The children did not look up as he walked through the living room. In the kitchen, Doreen, dressed for work, was eating scrambled eggs and bacon.

"What are you doing?" Earl said.

She continued to chew the food, cheeks puffed. But then she spit everything into a napkin.

"I couldn't help myself," she said.

"Slob," Earl said. "*Go ahead, eat! Go on!*" He went to the bedroom, closed the door, and lay on the covers. He could still hear the television. He put his hands behind his head and stared at the ceiling.

She opened the door.

"I'm going to try again," Doreen said.

"Okay," he said.

Two mornings later she called him into the bathroom. "Look," she said.

He read the scale. He opened a drawer and took out the paper and read the scale again while she grinned.

"Three-quarters of a pound," she said.

"It's something," he said and patted her hip.

He read the classifieds. He went to the state employment office. Every three or four days he drove someplace for an interview, and at night he counted her tips. He smoothed out the dollar bills on the table and stacked the nickels, dimes, and quarters in piles of one dollar each. Each morning he put her on the scale.

In two weeks she had lost three and a half pounds.

"I pick," she said. "I starve myself all day, and then I pick at work. It adds up."

But a week later she had lost five pounds. The week after that, nine and a half pounds. Her clothes were loose on her. She had to cut into the rent money to buy a new uniform.

"People are saying things at work," she said.

"What kind of things?" Earl said.

"That I'm too pale, for one thing," she said. "That I don't look like myself. They're afraid I'm losing too much weight."

"What is wrong with losing?" he said. "Don't you pay any attention to them. Tell them to mind their own business. They're not your husband. You don't have to live with them."

"I have to work with them," Doreen said.

"That's right," Earl said. "But they're not your husband."

Each morning he followed her into the bathroom and waited while she stepped onto the scale. He got down on his knees with a pencil and the piece of paper. The paper was covered with dates, days of the week, numbers. He read the number on the scale, consulted the paper, and either nodded his head or pursed his lips.

Doreen spent more time in bed now. She went back to bed after the children had left for school, and she napped in the afternoons before going to work. Earl helped around the house, watched television, and let her sleep. He did all the shopping, and once in a while he went on an interview.

One night he put the children to bed, turned off the television, and decided to go for a few drinks. When the bar closed, he drove to the coffee shop.

He sat at the counter and waited. When she saw him, she said, "Kids okay?"

Earl nodded.

He took his time ordering. He kept looking at her as she moved up and down behind the counter. He finally ordered a cheeseburger. She gave the order to the cook and went to wait on someone else.

Another waitress came by with a coffeepot and filled Earl's cup.

"Who's your friend?" he said and nodded at his wife.

"Her name's Doreen," the waitress said.

"She looks a lot different than the last time I was in here," he said.

"I wouldn't know," the waitress said.

He ate the cheeseburger and drank the coffee. People kept sitting down and getting up at the counter. Doreen waited on most of the people at the counter, though now and then the other waitress came along to take an order. Earl watched his wife and listened carefully. Twice he had to leave his place to go to the bathroom. Each time he wondered if he might have missed hearing something. When he came back the second time, he found his cup gone and someone in his place. He took a stool at the end of the counter next to an older man in a striped shirt.

"What do you want?" Doreen said to Earl when she saw him again. "Shouldn't you be home?"

"Give me some coffee," he said.

The man next to Earl was reading a newspaper. He looked up and watched Doreen pour Earl a cup of coffee. He glanced at Doreen as she walked away. Then he went back to his newspaper.

Earl sipped his coffee and waited for the man to say something. He watched the man out of the corner of his eye. The man had finished eating and his plate was pushed to the side. The man lit a cigarette, folded the newspaper in front of him, and continued to read.

Doreen came by and removed the dirty plate and poured the man more coffee.

"What do you think of that?" Earl said to the man, nodding at Doreen as she moved down the counter. "Don't you think that's something special?"

The man looked up. He looked at Doreen and then at Earl, and then went back to his newspaper.

"Well, what do you think?" Earl said. "I'm asking. Does it look good or not? Tell me."

The man rattled the newspaper.

When Doreen started down the counter again, Earl nudged the man's shoulder and said, "I'm telling you something. Listen. Look at the ass on her. Now you watch this now. Could I have a chocolate sundae?" Earl called to Doreen.

She stopped in front of him and let out her breath. Then she turned and picked up a dish and the ice-cream dipper. She leaned over the freezer, reached down, and began to press the dipper into the ice cream. Earl looked at the man and winked as Doreen's skirt traveled up her thighs. But the man's eyes caught the eyes of the other waitress. And then the man put the newspaper under his arm and reached into his pocket.

The other waitress came straight to Doreen. "Who is this character?" she said.

"Who?" Doreen said and looked around with the ice-cream dish in her hand.

"Him," the other waitress said and nodded at Earl. "Who is this joker, anyway?"

Earl put on his best smile. He held it. He held it until he felt his face pulling out of shape.

But the other waitress just studied him, and Doreen began to shake her head slowly. The man had put some change beside his cup and stood up, but he too waited to hear the answer. They all stared at Earl.

"He's a salesman. He's my husband," Doreen said at last, shrugging. Then she put the unfinished chocolate sundae in front of him and went to total up his check.

Are You a Doctor?

In slippers, pajamas, and robe, he hurried out of the study when the telephone began to ring. Since it was past ten, the call would be his wife. She phoned – late like this, after a few drinks – each night when she was out of town. She was a buyer, and all this week she had been away on business.

"Hello, dear," he said. "Hello," he said again.

"Who is this?" a woman asked.

"Well, who is *this*?" he said. "What number do you want?"

"Just a minute," the woman said. "It's 273–8063."

"That's my number," he said. "How did you get it?"

"I don't know. It was written down on a piece of paper when I got in from work," the woman said.

"Who wrote it down?"

"I don't know," the woman said. "The sitter, I guess. It must be her."

"Well, I don't know how she got it," he said, "but it's my telephone number, and it's unlisted. I'd appreciate it if you'd just toss it away. Hello? Did you hear me?"

"Yes, I heard," the woman said.

"Is there anything else?" he said. "It's late and I'm busy." He hadn't meant to be curt, but one couldn't take chances. He sat down on the chair by the telephone and said, "I hadn't meant to be curt. I only meant that it's late, and I'm concerned how you happen to have my number." He pulled off his slipper and began massaging his foot, waiting.

"I don't know either," she said. "I told you I just found the number written down, no note or anything. I'll ask Annette – that's the sitter – when I see her tomorrow. I didn't mean to disturb you. I only just now found the note. I've been in the kitchen ever since I came in from work."

"It's all right," he said. "Forget it. Just throw it away or something and forget it. There's no problem, so don't worry." He moved the receiver from one ear to the other.

"You sound like a nice man," the woman said.

"Do I? Well, that's nice of you to say." He knew he should hang up now, but it was good to hear a voice, even his own, in the quiet room.

"Oh, yes," she said. "I can tell."

He let go his foot.

"What's your name, if you don't mind my asking?" she said.

"My name is Arnold," he said.

"And what's your first name?" she said.

"Arnold is my first name," he said.

"Oh, forgive me," she said. "Arnold is your *first* name. And your second name, Arnold? What's your second name?"

"I really must hang up," he said.

"Arnold, for goodness' sake, I'm Clara Holt. Now *your* name is Mr Arnold what?"

"Arnold Breit," he said and then quickly added, "Clara Holt. That's nice. But I really think I should hang up now, Miss Holt. I'm expecting a call."

"I'm sorry, Arnold. I didn't mean to take up your time," she said.

"That's all right," he said. "It's been nice talking with you."

"You're kind to say that, Arnold."

"Will you hold the phone a minute?" he said. "I have to check on something." He went into the study for a cigar, took a minute lighting it up with the desk lighter, then removed his glasses and looked at himself in the mirror over the fireplace. When he returned to the telephone, he was half afraid she might be off the line.

"Hello?"

"Hello, Arnold," she said.

"I thought you might have hung up."

"Oh no," she said.

"About your having my number," he said. "Nothing to worry about, I don't suppose. Just throw it away, I suppose."

"I will, Arnold," she said.

"Well, I must say goodbye, then."

"Yes, of course," she said. "I'll say good night now."

He heard her draw a breath.

"I know I'm imposing, Arnold, but do you think we could meet somewhere we could talk? Just for a few minutes?"

"I'm afraid that's impossible," he said.

"Just for a minute, Arnold. My finding your number and everything. I feel strongly about this, Arnold."

"I'm an old man," he said.

"Oh, you're not," she said.

"Really, I'm old," he said.

"Could we meet somewhere, Arnold? You see, I haven't told you everything. There's something else," the woman said.

"What do you mean?" he said. "What is this exactly? Hello?"

She had hung up.

When he was preparing for bed, his wife called, somewhat intoxicated, he could tell, and they chatted for a while, but he said nothing about the other call. Later, as he was turning the covers down, the telephone rang again.

He picked up the receiver. "Hello. Arnold Breit speaking."

"Arnold, I'm sorry we got cut off. As I was saying, I think it's important we meet."

The next afternoon as he put the key into the lock, he could hear the telephone ringing. He dropped his briefcase and, still in hat, coat, and gloves, hurried over to the table and picked up the receiver.

"Arnold, I'm sorry to bother you again," the woman said. "But you must come to my house tonight around nine or nine-thirty. Can you do that for me, Arnold?"

His heart moved when he heard her use his name. "I couldn't do that," he said.

"Please, Arnold," she said. "It's important or I wouldn't be asking. I can't leave the house tonight because Cheryl is sick with a cold and now I'm afraid for the boy."

"And your husband?" He waited.

"I'm not married," she said. "You will come, won't you?"

"I can't promise," he said.

"I implore you to come," she said and then quickly gave him the address and hung up.

"*I implore you to come*," he repeated, still holding the receiver. He slowly took off his gloves and then his coat. He felt he had to be careful. He

25

went to wash up. When he looked in the bathroom mirror, he discovered the hat. It was then that he made the decision to see her, and he took off his hat and glasses and soaped his face. He checked his nails.

"You're sure this is the right street?" he asked the driver.

"This is the street and there's the building," the driver said.

"Keep going," he said. "Let me out at the end of the block."

He paid the driver. Lights from the upper windows illuminated the balconies. He could see planters on the balustrades and here and there a piece of lawn furniture. At one balcony a large man in a sweatshirt leaned over the railing and watched him walk toward the door.

He pushed the button under C. HOLT. The buzzer sounded, and he stepped back to the door and entered. He climbed the stairs slowly, stopping to rest briefly at each landing. He remembered the hotel in Luxembourg, the five flights he and his wife had climbed so many years ago. He felt a sudden pain in his side, imagined his heart, imagined his legs folding under him, imagined a loud fall to the bottom of the stairs. He took out his handkerchief and wiped his forehead. Then he removed his glasses and wiped the lenses, waiting for his heart to quiet.

He looked down the hall. The apartment house was very quiet. He stopped at her door, removed his hat, and knocked lightly. The door opened a crack to reveal a plump little girl in pajamas.

"Are you Arnold Breit?" she said.

"Yes, I am," he said. "Is your mother home?"

"She said for you to come in. She said to tell you she went to the drugstore for some cough syrup and aspirin."

He shut the door behind him. "What is your name? Your mother told me, but I forgot."

When the girl said nothing, he tried again.

"What is your name? Isn't your name Shirley?"

"Cheryl," she said. "C-h-e-r-y-l."

"Yes, now I remember. Well, I was close, you must admit."

She sat on a hassock across the room and looked at him.

"So you're sick, are you?" he said.

She shook her head.

"Not sick?"

"No," she said.

26

He looked around. The room was lighted by a gold floor lamp that had a large ashtray and a magazine rack affixed to the pole. A television set stood against the far wall, the picture on, the volume low. A narrow hallway led to the back of the apartment. The furnace was turned up, the air close with a medicinal smell. Hairpins and rollers lay on the coffee table, a pink bathrobe lay on the couch.

He looked at the child again, then raised his eyes toward the kitchen and the glass doors that gave off the kitchen onto the balcony. The doors stood slightly ajar, and a little chill went through him as he recalled the large man in the sweatshirt.

"Mama went out for a minute," the child said, as if suddenly waking up.

He leaned forward on his toes, hat in hand, and stared at her. "I think I'd better go," he said.

A key turned in the lock, the door swung open, and a small, pale, freckled woman entered carrying a paper sack.

"Arnold! I'm glad to see you!" She glanced at him quickly, uneasily, and shook her head strangely from side to side as she walked to the kitchen with the sack. He heard a cupboard door shut. The child sat on the hassock and watched him. He leaned his weight first on one leg and then the other, then placed the hat on his head and removed it in the same motion as the woman reappeared.

"Are you a doctor?" she asked.

"No," he said, startled. "No, I am not."

"Cheryl is sick, you see. I've been out buying things. Why didn't you take the man's coat?" she said, turning to the child. "Please forgive her. We're not used to company."

"I can't stay," he said. "I really shouldn't have come."

"Please sit down," she said. "We can't talk like this. Let me give her some medicine first. Then we can talk."

"I really must go," he said. "From the tone of your voice, I thought there was something urgent. But I really must go." He looked down at his hands and was aware he had been gesturing feebly.

"I'll put on tea water," he heard her say, as if she hadn't been listening. "Then I'll give Cheryl her medicine, and then we can talk."

She took the child by the shoulders and steered her into the kitchen. He saw the woman pick up a spoon, open a bottle of something after scanning the label, and pour out two doses.

"Now, you say good night to Mr Breit, sweetness, and go to your room."

He nodded to the child and then followed the woman to the kitchen. He did not take the chair she indicated, but instead one that let him face the balcony, the hallway, and the small living room. "Do you mind if I smoke a cigar?" he asked.

"I don't mind," she said. "I don't think it will bother me, Arnold. Please do."

He decided against it. He put his hands on his knees and gave his face a serious expression.

"This is still very much of a mystery to me," he said. "It's quite out of the ordinary, I assure you."

"I understand, Arnold," she said. "You'd probably like to hear the story of how I got your number?"

"I would indeed," he said.

They sat across from each other waiting for the water to boil. He could hear the television. He looked around the kitchen and then out toward the balcony again. The water began to bubble.

"You were going to tell me about the number," he said.

"What, Arnold? I'm sorry," she said.

He cleared his throat. "Tell me how you acquired my number," he said.

"I checked with Annette. The sitter – but of course you know that. Anyway, she told me the phone rang while she was here and it was somebody wanting me. They left a number to call, and it was your number she took down. That's all I know." She moved a cup around in front of her. "I'm sorry I can't tell you any more."

"Your water is boiling," he said.

She put out spoons, milk, sugar and poured the steaming water over the tea bags.

He added sugar and stirred his tea. "You said it was urgent that I come."

"Oh, *that*, Arnold," she said, turning away. "I don't know what made me say that. I can't imagine what I was thinking."

"Then there's nothing?" he said.

"No. I mean *yes*." She shook her head. "What you said, I mean. Nothing."

"I see," he said. He went on stirring his tea. "It's unusual," he said after a time, almost to himself. "Quite unusual." He smiled weakly, then moved the cup to one side and touched his lips with the napkin.

"You aren't leaving?" she said.

"I must," he said. "I'm expecting a call at home."

"Not yet, Arnold."

She scraped her chair back and stood up. Her eyes were a pale green, set deep in her pale face and surrounded by what he had at first thought was dark makeup. Appalled at himself, knowing he would despise himself for it, he stood and put his arms clumsily around her waist. She let herself be kissed, fluttering and closing her eyelids briefly.

"It's late," he said, letting go, turning away unsteadily. "You've been very gracious. But I must be leaving, Mrs Holt. Thank you for the tea."

"You will come again, won't you, Arnold?" she said.

He shook his head.

She followed him to the door, where he held out his hand. He could hear the television. He was sure the volume had been turned up. He remembered the other child then – the *boy*. Where was he?

She took his hand, raised it quickly to her lips. "You mustn't forget me, Arnold."

"I won't," he said. "Clara. Clara Holt," he said.

"We had a good talk," she said. She picked at something, a hair, a thread, on his suit collar. "I'm very glad you came, and I feel certain you'll come again." He looked at her carefully, but she was staring past him now, as if she were trying to remember something. "Now – good night, Arnold," she said, and with that she shut the door, almost catching his overcoat.

"Strange," he said as he started down the stairs. He took a long breath when he reached the sidewalk and paused a moment to look back at the building. But he was unable to determine which balcony was hers. The large man in the sweatshirt moved slightly against the railing and continued looking down at him.

He began walking, hands deep in his coat pockets. When he reached home, the telephone was ringing. He stood very quietly in the middle of the room, holding the key between his fingers until the ringing stopped. Then, tenderly, he put a hand against his chest and felt, through the layers of clothes, his beating heart. After a time he made his way into the bedroom.

Almost immediately the telephone came alive again, and this time he answered it. "Arnold. Arnold Breit speaking," he said.

"Arnold? My, aren't we formal tonight!" his wife said, her voice strong, teasing. "I've been calling since nine. Out living it up, Arnold?"

He remained silent and considered her voice.

"Are you there, Arnold?" she said. "You don't sound like yourself."

The Father

The baby lay in a basket beside the bed, dressed in a white bonnet and sleeper. The basket had been newly painted and tied with ice blue ribbons and padded with blue quilts. The three little sisters and the mother, who had just gotten out of bed and was still not herself, and the grandmother all stood around the baby, watching it stare and sometimes raise its fist to its mouth. He did not smile or laugh, but now and then he blinked his eyes and flicked his tongue back and forth through his lips when one of the girls rubbed his chin.

The father was in the kitchen and could hear them playing with the baby.

"Who do you love, baby?" Phyllis said and tickled his chin.

"He loves us all," Phyllis said, "but he really loves Daddy because Daddy's a boy too!"

The grandmother sat down on the edge of the bed and said, "Look at its little arm! So fat. And those little fingers! Just like its mother."

"Isn't he sweet?" the mother said. "So healthy, my little baby." And bending over, she kissed the baby on its forehead and touched the cover over its arm. "We love him too."

"But who does he look like, who does he look like?" Alice cried, and they all moved up closer around the basket to see who the baby looked like.

"He has pretty eyes," Carol said.

"*All* babies have pretty eyes," Phyllis said.

"He has his grandfather's lips," the grandmother said. "Look at those lips."

"I don't know . . ." the mother said. "I wouldn't say."

"The nose! The nose!" Alice cried.

"What about his nose?" the mother asked.

"It looks like somebody's nose," the girl answered

"No, I don't know," the mother said. "I don't think so."

"Those lips . . ." the grandmother murmured. "Those little fingers . . ." she said, uncovering the baby's hand and spreading out its fingers.

"Who does the baby look like?"

"He doesn't look like anybody," Phyllis said. And they moved even closer.

"*I* know! *I* know!" Carol said. "He looks like *Daddy*!" Then they looked closer at the baby.

"But who does Daddy *look* like?" Phyllis asked.

"Who does Daddy *look* like?" Alice repeated, and they all at once looked through to the kitchen where the father was sitting at the table with his back to them.

"Why, nobody!" Phyllis said and began to cry a little.

"Hush," the grandmother said and looked away and then back at the baby.

"Daddy doesn't look like *anybody*!" Alice said.

"But he has to look like *somebody*," Phyllis said, wiping her eyes with one of the ribbons. And all of them except the grandmother looked at the father, sitting at the table.

He had turned around in his chair and his face was white and without expression.

Nobody Said Anything

I could hear them out in the kitchen. I couldn't hear what they were saying, but they were arguing. Then it got quiet and she started to cry. I elbowed George. I thought he would wake up and say something to them so they would feel guilty and stop. But George is such an asshole. He started kicking and hollering.

"Stop gouging me, you bastard," he said. "I'm going to tell!"

"You dumb chickenshit," I said. "Can't you wise up for once? They're fighting and Mom's crying. Listen."

He listened with his head off the pillow. "I don't care," he said and turned over toward the wall and went back to sleep. George is a royal asshole.

Later I heard Dad leave to catch his bus. He slammed the front door. She had told me before he wanted to tear up the family. I didn't want to listen.

After a while she came to call us for school. Her voice sounded funny – I don't know. I said I felt sick at my stomach. It was the first week in October and I hadn't missed any school yet, so what could she say? She looked at me, but it was like she was thinking of something else. George was awake and listening. I could tell he was awake by the way he moved in the bed. He was waiting to see how it turned out so he could make his move.

"All right." She shook her head. "I just don't know. Stay home, then. But no TV, remember that."

George reared up. "I'm sick too," he said to her. "I have a headache. He gouged me and kicked me all night. I didn't get to sleep at all."

"That's enough!" she said. "You are going to school, George! You're not going to stay here and fight with your brother all day. Now get up and get dressed. I mean it. I don't feel like another battle this morning."

George waited until she left the room. Then he climbed out over the foot of the bed. "You bastard," he said and yanked all the covers off me. He dodged into the bathroom.

"I'll kill you," I said but not so loud that she could hear.

I stayed in bed until George left for school. When she started to get ready for work, I asked if she would make a bed for me on the couch. I said I wanted to study. On the coffee table I had the Edgar Rice Burroughs books I had gotten for my birthday and my Social Studies book. But I didn't feel like reading. I wanted her to leave so I could watch TV.

She flushed the toilet.

I couldn't wait any longer. I turned the picture on without the volume. I went out to the kitchen where she had left her pack of weeds and shook out three. I put them in the cupboard and went back to the couch and started reading *The Princess of Mars*. She came out and glanced at the TV but didn't say anything. I had the book open. She poked at her hair in front of the mirror and then went into the kitchen. I looked back at the book when she came out.

"I'm late. Goodbye, sweetheart." She wasn't going to bring up the TV. Last night she'd said she wouldn't know what it meant any more to go to work without being "stirred up".

"Don't cook anything. You don't need to turn the burners on for a thing. There's tuna fish in the icebox if you feel hungry." She looked at me. "But if your stomach is sick, I don't think you should put anything on it. Anyway, you don't need to turn the burners on. Do you hear? You take that medicine, sweetheart, and I hope your stomach feels better by tonight. Maybe we'll all feel better by tonight."

She stood in the doorway and turned the knob. She looked as if she wanted to say something else. She wore the white blouse, the wide black belt, and the black skirt. Sometimes she called it her outfit, sometimes her uniform. For as long as I could remember, it was always hanging in the closet or hanging on the clothesline or getting washed out by hand at night or being ironed in the kitchen.

She worked Wednesdays through Sundays.

"Bye, Mom."

I waited until she had started the car and had it warm. I listened as she pulled away from the curb. Then I got up and turned the sound on loud and went for the weeds. I smoked one and beat off while I watched a show about doctors and nurses. Then I turned to the other channel. Then I turned off the TV. I didn't feel like watching.

* * *

I finished the chapter where Tars Tarkas falls for a green woman, only to see her get her head chopped off the next morning by this jealous brother-in-law. It was about the fifth time I had read it. Then I went to their bedroom and looked around. I wasn't after anything in particular unless it was rubbers again and though I had looked all over I had never found any. Once I found a jar of Vaseline at the back of a drawer. I knew it must have something to do with it, but I didn't know what. I studied the label and hoped it would reveal something, a description of what people did, or else about how you applied the Vaseline, that sort of thing. But it didn't. *Pure Petroleum Jelly*, that was all it said on the front label. But just reading that was enough to give you a boner. *An Excellent Aid in the Nursery*, it said on the back. I tried to make the connection between *Nursery* – the swings and slides, the sandboxes, monkeybars – and what went on in bed between them. I had opened the jar lots of times and smelled inside and looked to see how much had been used since last time. This time I passed up the *Pure Petroleum Jelly*. I mean, all I did was look to see the jar was still there. I went through a few drawers, not really expecting to find anything. I looked under the bed. Nothing anywhere. I looked in the jar in the closet where they kept the grocery money. There was no change, only a five and a one. They would miss that. Then I thought I would get dressed and walk to Birch Creek. Trout season was open for another week or so, but almost everybody had quit fishing. Everybody was just sitting around now waiting for deer and pheasant to open.

I got out my old clothes. I put wool socks over my regular socks and took my time lacing up the boots. I made a couple of tuna sandwiches and some double-decker peanut-butter crackers. I filled my canteen and attached the hunting knife and the canteen to my belt. As I was going out the door, I decided to leave a note. So I wrote: "Feeling better and going to Birch Creek. Back soon. R. 3:15." That was about four hours from now. And about fifteen minutes before George would come in from school. Before I left, I ate one of the sandwiches and had a glass of milk with it.

It was nice out. It was fall. But it wasn't cold yet except at night. At night they would light the smudgepots in the orchards and you would wake up in the morning with a black ring of stuff in your nose. But nobody said anything. They said the smudging kept the young pears from freezing, so it was all right.

To get to Birch Creek, you go to the end of our street where you hit Sixteenth Avenue. You turn left on Sixteenth and go up the hill past the cemetery and down to Lennox, where there is a Chinese restaurant. From the crossroads there, you can see the airport, and Birch Creek is below the airport. Sixteenth changes to View Road at the crossroads. You follow View for a little way until you come to the bridge. There are orchards on both sides of the road. Sometimes when you go by the orchards you see pheasants running down the rows, but you can't hunt there because you might get shot by a Greek named Matsos. I guess it is about a forty-minute walk all in all.

I was halfway down Sixteenth when a woman in a red car pulled onto the shoulder ahead of me. She rolled down the window on the passenger's side and asked if I wanted a lift. She was thin and had little pimples around her mouth. Her hair was up in curlers. But she was sharp enough. She had a brown sweater with nice boobs inside.

"Playing hooky?"

"Guess so."

"Want a ride?"

I nodded.

"Get in. I'm kind of in a hurry."

I put the fly rod and the creel on the back seat. There were a lot of grocery sacks from Mel's on the floorboards and back seat. I tried to think of something to say.

"I'm going fishing," I said. I took off my cap, hitched the canteen around so I could sit, and parked myself next to the window.

"Well, I never would have guessed." She laughed. She pulled back onto the road. "Where are you going? Birch Creek?"

I nodded again. I looked at my cap. My uncle had bought it for me in Seattle when he had gone to watch a hockey game. I couldn't think of anything more to say. I looked out the window and sucked my cheeks. You always see yourself getting picked up by this woman. You know you'll fall for each other and that she'll take you home with her and let you screw her all over the house. I began to get a boner thinking about it. I moved the cap over my lap and closed my eyes and tried to think about baseball.

"I keep saying that one of these days I'll take up fishing," she said.

"They say it's very relaxing. I'm a nervous person."

I opened my eyes. We were stopped at the crossroads. I wanted to say, *Are you real busy? Would you like to start this morning?* But I was afraid to look at her.

"Will this help you? I have to turn here. I'm sorry I'm in a hurry this morning," she said.

"That's okay. This is fine." I took my stuff out. Then I put my cap on and took it off again while I talked. "Goodbye. Thanks. Maybe next summer," but I couldn't finish.

"You mean fishing? Sure thing." She waved with a couple of fingers the way women do.

I started walking, going over what I should have said. I could think of a lot of things. What was wrong with me? I cut the air with the fly rod and hollered two or three times. What I should have done to start things off was ask if we could have lunch together. No one was home at my house. Suddenly we are in my bedroom under the covers. She asks me if she can keep her sweater on and I say it's okay with me. She keeps her pants on too. That's all right, I say. I don't mind.

A Piper Cub dipped low over my head as it came in for a landing. I was a few feet from the bridge. I could hear the water running. I hurried down the embankment, unzipped, and shot off five feet over the creek. It must have been a record. I took a while eating the other sandwich and the peanut-butter crackers. I drank up half the water in the canteen. Then I was ready to fish.

I tried to think where to start. I had fished here for three years, ever since we had moved. Dad used to bring George and me in the car and wait for us, smoking, baiting our hooks, tying up new rigs for us if we snagged. We always started at the bridge and moved down, and we always caught a few. Once in a while, at the first of the season, we caught the limit. I rigged up and tried a few casts under the bridge first.

Now and then I cast under a bank or else in behind a big rock. But nothing happened. One place where the water was still and the bottom full of yellow leaves, I looked over and saw a few crawdads crawling there with their big ugly pinchers raised. Some quail flushed out of a brush pile. When I threw a stick, a rooster pheasant jumped up cackling about ten feet away and I almost dropped the rod.

The creek was slow and not very wide. I could walk across almost anywhere without it going over my boots. I crossed a pasture full of cow pads and came to where the water flowed out of a big pipe. I knew there was a little hole below the pipe, so I was careful. I got down on my knees when I was close enough to drop the line. It had just touched the water when I got a strike, but I missed him. I felt him roll with it. Then he was gone and the line flew back. I put another salmon egg on and tried a few more casts. But I knew I had jinxed it.

I went up the embankment and climbed under a fence that had a KEEP OUT sign on the post. One of the airport runways started here. I stopped to look at some flowers growing in the cracks in the pavement. You could see where the tires had smacked down on the pavement and left oily skid marks all around the flowers. I hit the creek again on the other side and fished along for a little way until I came to the hole. I thought this was as far as I would go. When I had first been up here three years ago, the water was roaring right up to the top of the banks. It was so swift then that I couldn't fish. Now the creek was about six feet below the bank. It bubbled and hopped through this little run at the head of the pool where you could hardly see bottom. A little farther down, the bottom sloped up and got shallow again as if nothing had happened. The last time I was up here I caught two fish about ten inches long and turned one that looked twice as big – a summer steelhead, Dad said when I told him about it. He said they come up during the high water in early spring but that most of them return to the river before the water gets low.

I put two more shot on the line and closed them with my teeth. Then I put a fresh salmon egg on and cast out where the water dropped over a shelf into the pool. I let the current take it down. I could feel the sinkers tap-tapping on rocks, a different kind of tapping than when you are getting a bite. Then the line tightened and the current carried the egg into sight at the end of the pool.

I felt lousy to have come this far up for nothing. I pulled out all kinds of line this time and made another cast. I laid the fly rod over a limb and lit the next to last weed. I looked up the valley and began to think about the woman. We were going to her house because she wanted help carrying in the groceries. Her husband was overseas. I touched her and she started shaking. We were French-kissing on the couch when she excused herself to go to the bathroom. I followed her. I watched as she pulled

down her pants and sat on the toilet. I had a big boner and she waved
me over with her hand. Just as I was going to unzip, I heard a plop in
the creek. I looked and saw the tip of my fly rod jiggling.

He wasn't very big and didn't fight much. But I played him as long as I
could. He turned on his side and lay in the current down below. I didn't
know what he was. He looked strange. I tightened the line and lifted him
over the bank into the grass, where he started wiggling. He was a trout.
But he was green. I never saw one like him before. He had green sides
with black trout spots, a greenish head, and like a green stomach. He
was the color of moss, that color green. It was as if he had been wrapped
up in moss a long time, and the color had come off all over him. He was
fat, and I wondered why he hadn't put up more of a fight. I wondered
if he was all right. I looked at him for a time longer, then I put him out
of his pain.

I pulled some grass and put it in the creel and laid him in there on the
grass.

I made some more casts, and then I guessed it must be two or three
o'clock. I thought I had better move down to the bridge. I thought I
would fish below the bridge awhile before I started home. And I decided
I would wait until night before I thought about the woman again. But
right away I got a boner thinking about the boner I would get that
night. Then I thought I had better stop doing it so much. About a month
back, a Saturday when they were all gone, I had picked up the Bible
right after and promised and swore I wouldn't do it again. But I got jism
on the Bible, and the promising and swearing lasted only a day or two,
until I was by myself again.

I didn't fish on the way down. When I got to the bridge, I saw a bicycle
in the grass. I looked and saw a kid about George's size running down the
bank. I started in his direction. Then he turned and started toward me,
looking in the water.

"Hey, what is it!" I hollered. "What's wrong?" I guessed he didn't hear
me. I saw his pole and fishing bag on the bank, and I dropped my stuff.
I ran over to where he was. He looked like a rat or something. I mean,
he had buckteeth and skinny arms and this ragged long-sleeved shirt
that was too small for him.

"God, I swear there's the biggest fish here I ever saw!" he called. "Hurry! Look! Look here! Here he is!"

I looked where he pointed and my heart jumped.

It was as long as my arm.

"God, oh God, will you look at him!" the boy said.

I kept looking. It was resting in a shadow under a limb that hung over the water. "God almighty," I said to the fish, "where did you come from?"

"What'll we do?" the boy said. "I wish I had my gun."

"We're going to get him," I said. "God, look at him! Let's get him into the riffle."

"You want to help me, then? We'll work it together!" the kid said.

The big fish had drifted a few feet downstream and lay there finning slowly in the clear water.

"Okay, what do we do?" the kid said.

"I can go up and walk down the creek and start him moving," I said. "You stand in the riffle, and when he tries to come through, you kick the living shit out of him. Get him onto the bank someway, I don't care how. Then get a good hold of him and hang on."

"Okay. Oh shit, look at him! Look, he's going! Where's he going?" the boy screamed.

I watched the fish move up the creek again and stop close to the bank. "He's not going anyplace. There's no place for him to go. See him? He's scared shitless. He knows we're here. He's just cruising around now looking for someplace to go. See, he stopped again. He can't go anyplace. He knows that. He knows we're going to nail him. He knows it's tough shit. I'll go up and scare him down. You get him when he comes through."

"I wish I had my gun," the boy said. "That would take care of him," the boy said.

I went up a little way, then started wading down the creek. I watched ahead of me as I went. Suddenly the fish darted away from the bank, turned right in front of me in a big cloudy swirl, and barrel-assed downstream.

"Here he comes!" I hollered. "Hey, hey, here he comes!" But the fish spun around before it reached the riffle and headed back. I splashed and hollered, and it turned again. "He's coming! Get him, get him! Here he comes!"

But the dumb idiot had himself a club, the asshole, and when the fish hit the riffle, the boy drove at him with the club instead of trying to kick the son of a bitch out like he should have. The fish veered off, going crazy, shooting on his side through the shallow water. He made it. The asshole idiot kid lunged for him and fell flat.

He dragged up onto the bank sopping wet. "I hit him!" the boy hollered. "I think he's hurt, too. I had my hands on him, but I couldn't hold him."

"You didn't have anything!" I was out of breath. I was glad the kid fell in. "You didn't even come close, asshole. What were you doing with that club? You should have kicked him. He's probably a mile away by now." I tried to spit. I shook my head. "I don't know. We haven't got him yet. We just may not get him," I said.

"Goddamn it, I hit him!" the boy screamed. "Didn't you see? I hit him, and I had my hands on him too. How close did you get? Besides, whose fish is it?" He looked at me. Water ran down his trousers over his shoes.

I didn't say anything else, but I wondered about that myself. I shrugged. "Well, okay. I thought it was both ours. Let's get him this time. No goof-ups, either one of us," I said.

We waded downstream. I had water in my boots, but the kid was wet up to his collar. He closed his buckteeth over his lip to keep his teeth from chattering.

The fish wasn't in the run below the riffle, and we couldn't see him in the next stretch, either. We looked at each other and began to worry that the fish really had gone far enough downstream to reach one of the deep holes. But then the goddamn thing rolled near the bank, actually knocking dirt into the water with his tail, and took off again. He went through another riffle, his big tail sticking out of the water. I saw him cruise over near the bank and stop, his tail half out of the water, finning just enough to hold against the current.

"Do you see him?" I said. The boy looked. I took his arm and pointed his finger. "Right *there*. Okay now, listen. I'll go down to that little run between those banks. See where I mean? You wait here until I give you a signal. Then you start down. Okay? And this time don't let him get by you if he heads back."

"Yeah," the boy said and worked his lip with those teeth. "Let's get him this time," the boy said, a terrible look of cold in his face.

I got up on the bank and walked down, making sure I moved quiet. I slid off the bank and waded in again. But I couldn't see the great big son of a bitch and my heart turned. I thought it might have taken off already. A little farther downstream and it would get to one of the holes. We would never get him then.

"He still there?" I hollered. I held my breath.

The kid waved.

"Ready!" I hollered again.

"Here goes!" the kid hollered back.

My hands shook. The creek was about three feet wide and ran between dirt banks. The water was low but fast. The kid was moving down the creek now, water up to his knees, throwing rocks ahead of him, splashing and shouting.

"Here he comes!" The kid waved his arms. I saw the fish now; it was coming right at me. He tried to turn when he saw me, but it was too late. I went down on my knees, grasping in the cold water. I scooped him with my hands and arms, up, up, raising him, throwing him out of the water, both of us falling onto the bank. I held him against my shirt, him flopping and twisting, until I could get my hands up his slippery sides to his gills. I ran one hand in and clawed through to his mouth and locked around his jaw. I knew I had him. He was still flopping and hard to hold, but I had him and I wasn't going to let go.

"We got him!" the boy hollered as he splashed up. "We got him, by God! Ain't he something! Look at him! Oh God, let me hold him," the boy hollered.

"We got to kill him first," I said. I ran my other hand down the throat. I pulled back on the head as hard as I could, trying to watch out for the teeth, and felt the heavy crunching. He gave a long slow tremble and was still. I laid him on the bank and we looked at him. He was at least two feet long, queerly skinny, but bigger than anything I had ever caught. I took hold of his jaw again.

"Hey," the kid said but didn't say any more when he saw what I was going to do. I washed off the blood and laid the fish back on the bank.

"I want to show him to my dad so bad," the kid said.

We were wet and shivering. We looked at him, kept touching him. We pried open his big mouth and felt his rows of teeth. His sides were scarred, whitish welts as big as quarters and kind of puffy. There were nicks out of his head around his eyes and on his snout where I guess he had banged into the rocks and been in fights. But he was so skinny, too skinny for how long he was, and you could hardly see the pink stripe down his sides, and his belly was gray and slack instead of white and solid like it should have been. But I thought he was something.

"I guess I'd better go pretty soon," I said. I looked at the clouds over the hills where the sun was going down. "I better get home."

"I guess so. Me too. I'm freezing," the kid said. "Hey, I want to carry him," the kid said.

"Let's get a stick. We'll put it through his mouth and both carry him," I said.

The kid found a stick. We put it through the gills and pushed until the fish was in the middle of the stick. Then we each took an end and started back, watching the fish as he swung on the stick.

"What are we going to do with him?" the kid said.

"I don't know," I said. "I guess I caught him," I said.

"We both did. Besides, I saw him first."

"That's true," I said. "Well, you want to flip for him or what?" I felt with my free hand, but I didn't have any money. And what would I have done if I had lost?

Anyway, the kid said, "No, let's not flip."

I said, "All right. It's okay with me." I looked at that boy, his hair standing up, his lips gray. I could have taken him if it came to that. But I didn't want to fight.

We got to where we had left our things and picked up our stuff with one hand, neither of us letting go of his end of the stick. Then we walked up to where his bicycle was. I got a good hold on the stick in case the kid tried something.

Then I had an idea. "We could half him," I said.

"What do you mean?" the boy said, his teeth chattering again. I could feel him tighten his hold on the stick.

"Half him. I got a knife. We cut him in two and each take half. I don't know, but I guess we could do that."

He pulled at a piece of his hair and looked at the fish. "You going to use that knife?"

"You got one?" I said.

The boy shook his head.

"Okay," I said.

I pulled the stick out and laid the fish in the grass beside the kid's bicycle. I took out the knife. A plane taxied down the runway as I measured a line. "Right here?" I said. The kid nodded. The plane roared down the runway and lifted up right over our heads. I started cutting down into him. I came to his guts and turned him over and stripped everything out. I kept cutting until there was only a flap of skin on his belly holding him together. I took the halves and worked them in my hands and I tore him in two.

I handed the kid the tail part.

"No," he said, shaking his head. "I want that half."

I said, "They're both the same! Now goddamn, watch it, I'm going to get mad in a minute."

"I don't care," the boy said. "If they're both the same, I'll take that one. They're both the same, right?"

"They're both the same," I said. "But I think I'm keeping this half here. I did the cutting."

"I want it," the kid said. "I saw him first."

"Whose knife did we use?" I said.

"I don't want the tail," the kid said.

I looked around. There were no cars on the road and nobody else fishing. There was an airplane droning, and the sun was going down. I was cold all the way through. The kid was shivering hard, waiting.

"I got an idea," I said. I opened the creel and showed him the trout. "See? It's a green one. It's the only green one I ever saw. So whoever takes the head, the other guy gets the green trout and the tail part. Is that fair?"

The kid looked at the green trout and took it out of the creel and held it. He studied the halves of the fish.

"I guess so," he said. "Okay, I guess so. You take that half. I got more meat on mine."

"I don't care," I said. "I'm going to wash him off. Which way do you live?" I said.

"Down on Arthur Avenue." He put the green trout and his half of the fish into a dirty canvas bag. "Why?"

"Where's that? Is that down by the ball park?" I said.

"Yeah, but why, I said." That kid looked scared.

"I live close to there," I said. "So I guess I could ride on the handlebars. We could take turns pumping. I got a weed we could

44

smoke, if it didn't get wet on me."

But the kid only said, "I'm freezing."

I washed my half in the creek. I held his big head under water and opened his mouth. The stream poured into his mouth and out the other end of what was left of him.

"I'm freezing," the kid said.

I saw George riding his bicycle at the other end of the street. He didn't see me. I went around to the back to take off my boots. I unslung the creel so I could raise the lid and get set to march into the house, grinning.

I heard their voices and looked through the window. They were sitting at the table. Smoke was all over the kitchen. I saw it was coming from a pan on the burner. But neither of them paid any attention.

"What I'm telling you is the gospel truth," he said. "What do kids know? You'll see."

She said, "I'll see nothing. If I thought that, I'd rather see them dead first."

He said, "What's the matter with you? You better be careful what you say!"

She started to cry. He smashed out a cigarette in the ashtray and stood up.

"Edna, do you know this pan is burning up?" he said.

She looked at the pan. She pushed her chair back and grabbed the pan by its handle and threw it against the wall over the sink.

He said, "Have you lost your mind? Look what you've done!" He took a dish cloth and began to wipe up stuff from the pan.

I opened the back door. I started grinning. I said, "You won't believe what I caught at Birch Creek. Just look. Look here. Look at this. Look what I caught."

My legs shook. I could hardly stand. I held the creel out to her, and she finally looked in. "Oh, oh, my God! What is it? A snake! What is it? Please, please take it out before I throw up."

"Take it out!" he screamed. "Didn't you hear what she said? Take it out of here!" he screamed.

I said, "But look, Dad. Look what it is."

He said, "I don't want to look."

I said, "It's a gigantic summer steelhead from Birch Creek. Look! Isn't he something? It's a monster! I chased him up and down the creek like a madman!" My voice was crazy. But I could not stop. "There was another one, too," I hurried on. "A green one. I swear! It was green! Have you ever seen a green one?"

He looked into the creel and his mouth fell open.

He screamed, "Take that goddamn thing out of here! What in the hell is the matter with you? Take it the hell out of the kitchen and throw it in the goddamn garbage!"

I went back outside. I looked into the creel. What was there looked silver under the porch light. What was there filled the creel.

I lifted him out. I held him. I held that half of him.

Sixty Acres

The call had come an hour ago, when they were eating. Two men were shooting on Lee Waite's part of Toppenish Creek, down below the bridge on the Cowiche Road. It was the third or fourth time this winter someone had been in there, Joseph Eagle reminded Lee Waite. Joseph Eagle was an old Indian who lived on his government allotment in a little place off the Cowiche Road, with a radio he listened to day and night and a telephone in case he got sick. Lee Waite wished the old Indian would let him be about that land, that Joseph Eagle would do something else about it, if he wanted, besides call.

Out on the porch, Lee Waite leaned on one leg and picked at a string of meat between his teeth. He was a small thin man with a thin face and long black hair. If it had not been for the phone call, he would have slept awhile this afternoon. He frowned and took his time pulling into his coat; they would be gone anyway when he got there. That was usually the way. The hunters from Toppenish or Yakima could drive the reservation roads like anyone else; they just weren't allowed to hunt. But they would cruise by that untenanted and irresistible sixty acres of his, two, maybe three times, then, if they were feeling reckless, park down off the road in the trees and hurry through the knee-deep barley and wild oats, down to the creek – maybe getting some ducks, maybe not, but always doing a lot of shooting in the little time before they cleared out. Joseph Eagle sat crippled in his house and watched them plenty of times. Or so he told Lee Waite.

He cleaned his teeth with his tongue and squinted in the late-afternoon winter half-light. He wasn't afraid; it wasn't that, he told himself. He just didn't want trouble.

The porch, small and built on just before the war, was almost dark. The one window glass had been knocked out years before, and Waite had nailed a beet sack over the opening. It hung there next to the cabinet, matted-

47

thick and frozen, moving slightly as the cold air from outside came in around the edges. The walls were crowded with old yokes and harnesses, and up on one side, above the window, was a row of rusted hand tools. He made a last sweep with his tongue, tightened the light bulb into the overhead socket, and opened the cabinet. He took out the old double-barrel from in back and reached into the box on the top shelf for a handful of shells. The brass ends of the shells felt cold, and he rolled them in his hand before dropping them into a pocket of the old coat he was wearing.

"Aren't you going to load it, Papa?" the boy Benny asked from behind.

Waite turned, saw Benny and little Jack standing in the kitchen doorway. Ever since the call they had been after him – had wanted to know if this time he was going to shoot somebody. It bothered him, kids talking like that, like they would enjoy it, and now they stood at the door, letting all the cold air in the house and looking at the large gun up under his arm.

"Get back in that house where the hell you belong," he said.

They left the door open and ran back in where his mother and Nina were and on through to the bedroom. He could see Nina at the table trying to coax bites of squash into the baby, who was pulling back and shaking her head. Nina looked up, tried to smile.

Waite stepped into the kitchen and shut the door, leaned against it. She was plenty tired, he could tell. A beaded line of moisture glistened over her lip, and, as he watched, she stopped to move the hair away from her forehead. She looked up at him again, then back at the baby. It had never bothered her like this when she was carrying before. The other times she could hardly sit still and used to jump up and walk around, even if there wasn't much to do except cook a meal or sew. He fingered the loose skin around his neck and glanced covertly at his mother, dozing since the meal in a chair by the stove. She squinted her eyes at him and nodded. She was seventy and shriveled, but her hair was still crow-black and hung down in front over her shoulders in two long tight braids. Lee Waite was sure she had something wrong with her because sometimes she went two days without saying something, just sitting in the other room by the window and staring off up the valley. It made him shiver when she did that, and he didn't know any more what her little signs and signals, her silences, were supposed to mean.

"Why don't you say something?" he asked, shaking his head. "How do I know what you mean, Mama, if you don't say?" Waite looked at her for a minute and watched her tug at the ends of her braids, waited for her to say something. Then he grunted and crossed by in front of her, took his hat off a nail, and went out.

It was cold. An inch or two of grainy snow from three days past covered everything, made the ground lumpy, and gave a foolish look to the stripped rows of beanpoles in front of the house. The dog came scrabbling out from under the house when it heard the door, started off for the truck without looking back. "Come here!" Waite called sharply, his voice looping in the thin air.

Leaning over, he took the dog's cold, dry muzzle in his hand. "You better stay here this time. Yes, yes." He flapped the dog's ear back and forth and looked around. He could not see the Satus Hills across the valley because of the heavy overcast, just the wavy flatness of sugar-beet fields – white, except for black places here and there where the snow had not gotten. One place in sight – Charley Treadwell's, a long way off – but no lights lit that he could tell. Not a sound anywhere, just the low ceiling of heavy clouds pressing down on everything. He'd thought there was a wind, but it was still.

"Stay here now. You hear?"

He started for the truck, wishing again he did not have to go. He had dreamed last night, again – about what he could not remember – but he'd had an uneasy feeling ever since he woke up. He drove in low gear down to the gate, got out and unhooked it, drove past, got out again and hooked it. He did not keep horses any more – but it was a habit he had gotten into, keeping the gate shut.

Down the road, the grader was scraping toward him, the blade shrieking fiercely every time the metal hit the frozen gravel. He was in no hurry, and he waited the long minutes it took the grader to come up. One of the men in the cab leaned out with a cigarette in his hand and waved as they went by. But Waite looked off. He pulled out onto the road after they passed. He looked over at Charley Treadwell's when he went by, but there were still no lights, and the car was gone. He remembered what Charley had told him a few days ago, about a fight Charley had had last Sunday with some kid who came over his fence in the afternoon and shot into a pond of ducks, right down by the barn. The ducks came in there every afternoon, Charley said. They *trusted* him, he said, as if that mattered. He'd run down from the barn where he was milking, waving his arms and shouting, and the kid had pointed the gun at him. If I could've just got that gun away from him, Charley had said, staring hard at Waite with his one good eye and nodding slowly. Waite hitched a little in the seat. He did not want any trouble like that. He hoped whoever it was would be gone when he got there, like the other times.

Out to the left he passed Fort Simcoe, the white-painted tops of the old buildings standing behind the reconstructed palisade. The gates of the place were open, and Lee Waite could see cars parked around inside and a few people in coats, walking. He never bothered to stop. Once the teacher had brought all the kids out here – a field trip, she called it – but Waite had stayed home from school that day. He rolled down the window and cleared his throat, hawked it at the gate as he passed.

He turned onto Lateral B and then came to Joseph Eagle's place – all the lights on, even the porch light. Waite drove past, down to where the Cowiche Road came in, and got out of the truck and listened. He had begun to think they might be gone and he could turn around and go on back when he heard a grouping of dull far-off shots come across the fields. He waited awhile, then took a rag and went around the truck and tried to wipe off some of the snow and ice in the window edges. He kicked the snow off his shoes before getting in, drove a little farther until he could see the bridge, then looked for the tracks that turned off into the trees, where he knew he would find their car. He pulled in behind the gray sedan and switched the ignition off.

He sat in the truck and waited, squeaking his foot back and forth on the brake and hearing them shoot every now and then. After a few minutes he couldn't sit still any longer and got out, walked slowly around to the front. He had not been down there to do anything in four or five years. He leaned against the fender and looked out over the land. He could not understand where all the time had gone.

He remembered when he was little, wanting to grow up. He used to come down here often then and trap this part of the creek for muskrat and set night-lines for German brown. Waite looked around, moved his feet inside his shoes. All that was a long time ago. Growing up, he had heard his father say he intended this land for the three boys. But both brothers had been killed. Lee Waite was the one it came down to, all of it.

He remembered: deaths. Jimmy first. He remembered waking to the tremendous pounding on the door – dark, the smell of wood pitch from the stove, an automobile outside with the lights on and the motor running, and a crackling voice coming from a speaker inside. His father throws open the door, and the enormous figure of a man in a cowboy hat and wearing a gun – the deputy sheriff – fills the doorway. *Waite? Your boy Jimmy been stabbed at a dance in Wapato.* Everyone had gone away in the truck and Lee was left by himself. He had crouched, alone the rest of the night, in front of the wood stove, watching the shadows jump across the wall. Later, when he was twelve, another one came, a different sheriff, and only said they'd better come along.

He pushed off from the truck and walked the few feet over to the edge of the field. Things were different now, that's all there was to it. He was thirty-two, and Benny and little Jack were growing up. And there was the baby. Waite shook his head. He closed his hand around one of the tall stalks of milkweed. He snapped its neck and looked up when he heard the soft chuckling of ducks overhead. He wiped his hand on his pants and followed them for a moment, watched them set their wings at the same instant and circle once over the creek. Then they flared. He saw three ducks fall before he heard the shots. He turned abruptly and started back for the truck.

He took out his gun, careful not to slam the door. He moved into the trees. It was almost dark. He coughed once and then stood with his lips pressed together.

They came thrashing through the brush, two of them. Then, jiggling and squeaking the fence, they climbed over into the field and crunched through the snow. They were breathing hard by the time they got up close to the car.

"My God, there's a truck there!" one of them said and dropped the ducks he was carrying.

It was a boy's voice. He had on a heavy hunting coat, and in the game pockets Waite could dimly make out the enormous padding of ducks.

"Take it easy, will you!" The other boy stood craning his head around, trying to see. "Hurry up! There's nobody inside. Get the hell in the car!"

Not moving, trying to keep his voice steady, Waite said, "Stand there. Put your guns right there on the ground." He edged out of the trees and faced them, raised and lowered his gun barrels. "Take off them coats now and empty them out."

"Oh God! *God* almighty!" one of them said.

The other did not say anything but took off his coat and began pulling out the ducks, still looking around.

Waite opened the door of their car, fumbled an arm around inside until he found the headlights. The boys put a hand up to shield their eyes, then turned their backs to the light.

"Whose land do you think this is?" Waite said. "What do you mean, shooting ducks on my land!"

One boy turned around cautiously, his hand still in front of his eyes. "What are you going to do?"

"What do you think I'm going to do?" Waite said. His voice sounded strange to him, light, insubstantial. He could hear the ducks settling on the creek, chattering to other ducks still in the air. "What do you think I'm going to do with you?" he said. "What would you do if you caught boys trespassing on your land?"

"If they said they was sorry and it was the first time, I'd let them go," the boy answered.

"I would too, sir, if they said they was sorry," the other boy said.

"You would? You really think that's what you'd do?" Waite knew he was stalling for time.

They did not answer. They stood in the glare of the headlights and then turned their backs again.

"How do I know you wasn't here before?" Waite said. "The other times I had to come down here?"

"Word of honor, sir, we never been here before. We just drove by. For godsake," the boy sobbed.

"That's the whole truth," the other boy said. "Anybody can make a mistake once in his life."

It was dark now, and a thin drizzle was coming down in front of the lights. Waite turned up his collar and stared at the boys. From down on the creek the strident quacking of a drake carried up to him. He glanced around at the awful shapes of the trees, then back at the boys again.

"Maybe so," he said and moved his feet. He knew he would let them go in a minute. There wasn't much else he could do. He was putting them off the land; that was what mattered. "What's your names, anyway?

What's yours? You. Is this here your car or not? What's your name?"

"Bob Roberts," the one boy answered quickly and looked sideways at the other.

"Williams, sir," the other boy said. "Bill Williams, sir."

Waite was willing to understand that they were kids, that they were lying to him because they were afraid. They stood with their backs to him, and Waite stood looking at them.

"You're lying!" he said, shocking himself. "Why you lying to me? You come onto my land and shoot my ducks and then you lie like hell to me!" He laid the gun over the car door to steady the barrels. He could hear branches rubbing in the treetops. He thought of Joseph Eagle sitting up there in his lighted house, his feet on a box, listening to the radio.

"All right, all right," Waite said. "Liars! Just stand there, liars." He walked stiffly around to his truck and got out an old beet sack, shook it open, had them put all the ducks in that. When he stood still, waiting, his knees unaccountably began to shake.

"Go ahead and go. Go on!"

He stepped back as they came up to the car. "I'll back up to the road. You back up along with me."

"Yes, sir," the one boy said as he slid in behind the wheel. "But what if I can't get this thing started now? The battery might be dead, you know. It wasn't very strong to begin with."

"I don't know," Waite said. He looked around. "I guess I'd have to push you out."

The boy shut off the lights, stamped on the accelerator, and hit the starter. The engine turned over slowly but caught, and the boy held his foot down on the pedal and raced the engine before firing up the lights again. Waite studied their pale cold faces staring out at him, looking for a sign from him.

He slung the bag of ducks into his truck and slid the double-barrel across the seat. He got in and backed out carefully onto the road. He waited until they were out, then followed them down to Lateral B and stopped with his motor running, watching their taillights disappear toward Toppenish. He had put them off the land. That was all that mattered. Yet he could not understand why he felt something crucial had happened, a failure.

But nothing had happened.

* * *

Patches of fog had blown in from down the valley. He couldn't see much over toward Charley's when he stopped to open the gate, only a faint light burning out on the porch that Waite did not remember seeing that afternoon. The dog waited on its belly by the barn, jumped up and began snuffling the ducks as Waite swung them over his shoulder and started up to the house. He stopped on the porch long enough to put the gun away. The ducks he left on the floor beside the cabinet. He would clean them tomorrow or the next day.

"Lee?" Nina called.

Waite took off his hat, loosened the light bulb, and before opening the door he paused a moment in the quiet dark.

Nina was at the kitchen table, the little box with her sewing things beside her on another chair. She held a piece of denim in her hand. Two or three of his shirts were on the table, along with a pair of scissors. He pumped a cup of water and picked up from a shelf over the sink some of the colored rocks the kids were always bringing home. There was a dry pine cone there too and a few big papery maple leaves from the summer. He glanced in the pantry. But he was not hungry. Then he walked over to the doorway and leaned against the jamb.

It was a small house. There was no place to go.

In the back, in one room, all of the children slept, and in the room off from this, Waite and Nina and his mother slept, though sometimes, in the summer, Waite and Nina slept outside. There was never a place to go. His mother was still sitting beside the stove, a blanket over her legs now and her tiny eyes open, watching him.

"The boys wanted to stay up until you came back," Nina said, "but I told them you said they had to go to bed."

"Yes, that's right," he said. "They had to go to bed, all right."

"I was afraid," she said.

"Afraid?" He tried to make it sound as if this surprised him. "Were you afraid too, Mama?"

The old woman did not answer. Her fingers fiddled around the sides of the blanket, tucking and pulling, covering against draft.

"How do you feel, Nina? Feel any better tonight?" He pulled out a chair and sat down by the table.

His wife nodded. He said nothing more, only looked down and

began scoring his thumbnail into the table.

"Did you catch who it was?" she said.

"It was two kids," he said. "I let them go."

He got up and walked to the other side of the stove, spat into the woodbox, and stood with his fingers hooked into his back pockets. Behind the stove the wood was black and peeling, and overhead he could see, sticking out from a shelf, the brown mesh of a gill net wrapped around the prongs of a salmon spear. But what was it? He squinted at it.

"I let them go," he said. "Maybe I was easy on them."

"You did what was right," Nina said.

He glanced over the stove at his mother. But there was no sign from her, only the black eyes staring at him.

"I don't know," he said. He tried to think about it, but already it seemed as if it had happened, whatever it was, long ago. "I should've given them more of a scare, I guess." He looked at Nina. "My land," he added. "I could've killed them."

"Kill who?" his mother said.

"Them kids down on the Cowiche Road land. What Joseph Eagle called about."

From where he stood he could see his mother's fingers working in her lap, tracing the raised design in the blanket. He leaned over the stove, wanting to say something else. But he did not know what.

He wandered to the table and sat down again. Then he realized he still had on his coat, and he got up, took a while unfastening it, and then laid it across the table. He pulled up the chair close to his wife's knees, crossed his arms limply, and took his shirt sleeves between his fingers.

"I was thinking maybe I'll lease out that land down there to the hunting clubs. No good to us down there like that. Is it? Our house was down there or it was our land right out here in front would be something different, right?"

In the silence he could hear only the wood snapping in the stove. He laid his hands flat on the table and could feel the pulse jumping in his arms. "I can lease it out to one of the duck clubs from Toppenish. Or Yakima. Any of them would be glad to get hold of land like that, right on the flyway. That's some of the best hunting land in the valley . . . If I could put it to some use someway, it would be different then." His voice trailed off.

She moved in the chair. She said, "If you think we should do it. It's whatever you think. I don't know."

"I don't know, either," he said. His eyes crossed the floor, raised past his mother, and again came to rest on the salmon spear. He got up, shaking his head. As he moved across the little room, the old woman crooked her head and laid her cheek on the chairback, eyes narrowed and following him. He reached up, worked the spear and the mass of netting off the splintery shelf, and turned around behind her chair. He looked at the tiny dark head, at the brown woolen shawl shaped smooth over the hunched shoulders. He turned the spear in his hands and began to unwrap the netting.

"How much would you get?" Nina said.

He knew he didn't know. It even confused him a little. He plucked at the netting, then placed the spear back on the shelf. Outside, a branch scraped roughly against the house.

"Lee?"

He was not sure. He would have to ask around. Mike Chuck had leased out thirty acres last fall for five hundred dollars. Jerome Shinpa leased some of his land every year, but Waite had never asked how much he got.

"Maybe a thousand dollars," he said.

"A thousand dollars?" she said.

He nodded, felt relief at her amazement. "Maybe so. Maybe more. I will have to see. I will have to ask somebody how much." It was a lot of money. He tried to think about having a thousand dollars. He closed his eyes and tried to think.

"That wouldn't be selling it, would it?" Nina asked. "If you lease it to them, that means it's still your land?"

"Yes, yes, it's still my land!" He went over to her and leaned across the table. "Don't you know the difference, Nina? They can't *buy* land on the reservation. Don't you know that? I will lease it to them for them to use."

"I see," she said. She looked down and picked at the sleeve of one of his shirts. "They will have to give it back? It will still belong to you?"

"Don't you understand?" he said. He gripped the table edge. "It is a lease!"

"What will Mama say?" Nina asked. "Will it be all right?"

They both looked over at the old woman. But her eyes were closed and she seemed to be sleeping.

"A thousand dollars," Nina said and shook her head.

A thousand dollars. Maybe more. He didn't know. But even a thousand dollars! He wondered how he would go about it, letting people know he had land to lease. It was too late now for this year – but he could start asking around in the spring. He crossed his arms and tried to think. His legs began to tremble, and he leaned against the wall. He rested there and then let his weight slide gently down the wall until he was squatting.

"It's just a lease," he said.

He stared at the floor. It seemed to slant in his direction; it seemed to move. He shut his eyes and brought his hands against his ears to steady himself. And then he thought to cup his palms, so that there would come that roaring, like the wind howling up from a seashell.

What's in Alaska?

Jack got off work at three. He left the station and drove to a shoe store near his apartment. He put his foot up on the stool and let the clerk unlace his work boot.

"Something comfortable," Jack said. "For casual wear."

"I have something," the clerk said.

The clerk brought out three pairs of shoes and Jack said he would take the soft beige-colored shoes that made his feet feel free and springy. He paid the clerk and put the box with his boots under his arm. He looked down at his new shoes as he walked. Driving home, he felt that his foot moved freely from pedal to pedal.

"You bought some new shoes," Mary said. "Let me see."

"Do you like them?" Jack said.

"I don't like the color, but I'll bet they're comfortable. You needed new shoes."

He looked at the shoes again. "I've got to take a bath," he said.

"We'll have an early dinner," she said. "Helen and Carl asked us over tonight. Helen got Carl a water pipe for his birthday and they're anxious to try it out." Mary looked at him. "Is it all right with you?"

"What time?"

"Around seven."

"It's all right," he said.

She looked at his shoes again and sucked her cheeks. "Take your bath," she said.

Jack ran the water and took off his shoes and clothes. He lay in the tub for a while and then used a brush to get at the lube grease under his nails. He dropped his hands and then raised them to his eyes.

She opened the bathroom door. "I brought you a beer," she said. Steam drifted around her and out into the living room.

"I'll be out in a minute," he said. He drank some of the beer.

She sat on the edge of the tub and put her hand on his thigh. "Home from the wars," she said.

"Home from the wars," he said.

She moved her hand through the wet hair on his thigh. Then she clapped her hands. "Hey, I have something to tell you! I had an interview today, and I think they're going to offer me a job – in *Fairbanks*."

"Alaska?" he said.

She nodded. "What do you think of that?"

"I've always wanted to go to Alaska. Does it look pretty definite?"

She nodded again. "They liked me. They said I'd hear next week."

"That's great. Hand me a towel, will you? I'm getting out."

"I'll go and set the table," she said.

His fingertips and toes were pale and wrinkled. He dried slowly and put on clean clothes and the new shoes. He combed his hair and went out to the kitchen. He drank another beer while she put dinner on the table.

"We're supposed to bring some cream soda and something to munch on," she said. "We'll have to go by the store."

"Cream soda and munchies. Okay," he said.

When they had eaten, he helped her clear the table. Then they drove to the market and bought cream soda and potato chips and corn chips and onion-flavored snack crackers. At the checkout counter he added a handful of U-No bars to the order.

"Hey, yeah," she said when she saw them.

They drove home again and parked, and then they walked the block to Helen and Carl's.

Helen opened the door. Jack put the sack on the dining-room table. Mary sat down in the rocking chair and sniffed.

"We're late," she said. "They started without us, Jack."

Helen laughed. "We had one when Carl came in. We haven't lighted the water pipe yet. We were waiting until you got here." She stood in the middle of the room, looking at them and grinning. "Let's see what's in the sack," she said. "Oh, wow! Say, I think I'll have one of these corn chips right now. You guys want some?"

"We just ate dinner," Jack said. "We'll have some pretty soon." Water had stopped running and Jack could hear Carl whistling in the bathroom

"We have some Popsicles and some M&Ms," Helen said. She stood beside the table and dug into the potato-chip bag. "If Carl ever gets out of the shower, he'll get the water pipe going." She opened the box of snack crackers and put one in her mouth. "Say, these are really good," she said.

"I don't know what Emily Post would say about you," Mary said.

Helen laughed. She shook her head.

Carl came out of the bathroom. "Hi, everybody. Hi, Jack. What's so funny?" he said, grinning. "I could hear you laughing."

"We were laughing at Helen," Mary said.

"Helen was just laughing," Jack said.

"She's funny," Carl said. "Look at the goodies! Hey, you guys ready for a glass of cream soda? I'll get the pipe going."

"I'll have a glass," Mary said. "What about you, Jack?"

"I'll have some," Jack said.

"Jack's on a little bummer tonight," Mary said.

"Why do you say that?" Jack asked. He looked at her. "That's a good way to put me on one."

"I was just teasing," Mary said. She came over and sat beside him on the sofa. "I was just teasing, honey."

"Hey, Jack, don't get on a bummer," Carl said. "Let me show you what I got for my birthday. Helen, open one of those bottles of cream soda while I get the pipe going. I'm real dry."

Helen carried the chips and crackers to the coffee table. Then she produced a bottle of cream soda and four glasses.

"Looks like we're going to have a party," Mary said.

"If I didn't starve myself all day, I'd put on ten pounds a week," Helen said.

"I know what you mean," Mary said.

Carl came out of the bedroom with the water pipe. "What do you think of this?" he said to Jack. He put the water pipe on the coffee table.

"That's really something," Jack said. He picked it up and looked at it.

"It's called a hookah," Helen said. "That's what they called it where I bought it. It's just a little one, but it does the job." She laughed.

"Where did you get it?" Mary said.

"What? That little place on Fourth Street. You know," Helen said.

"Sure. I know," Mary said. "I'll have to go in there some day," Mary said. She folded her hands and watched Carl.

"How does it work?" Jack said.

"You put the stuff here," Carl said. "And you light this. Then you inhale through this here and the smoke is filtered through the water. It has a good taste to it and it really hits you."

"I'd like to get Jack one for Christmas," Mary said. She looked at Jack and grinned and touched his arm.

"I'd like to have one," Jack said. He stretched his legs and looked at his shoes under the light.

"Here, try this," Carl said, letting out a thin stream of smoke and passing the tube to Jack. "See if this isn't okay."

Jack drew on the tube, held the smoke, and passed the tube to Helen.

"Mary first," Helen said. "I'll go after Mary. You guys have to catch up."

"I won't argue," Mary said. She slipped the tube in her mouth and drew rapidly, twice, and Jack watched the bubbles she made.

"That's really okay," Mary said. She passed the tube to Helen.

"We broke it in last night," Helen said, and laughed loudly.

"She was still stoned when she got up with the kids this morning," Carl said, and he laughed. He watched Helen pull on the tube.

"How are the kids?" Mary asked.

"They're fine," Carl said and put the tube in his mouth. Jack sipped the cream soda and watched the bubbles in the pipe. They reminded him of bubbles rising from a diving helmet. He imagined a lagoon and schools of remarkable fish.

Carl passed the tube.

Jack stood up and stretched.

"Where are you going, honey?" Mary asked.

"No place," Jack said. He sat down and shook his head and grinned. "Jesus."

Helen laughed.

"What's funny?" Jack said after a long time.

"God, I don't know," Helen said. She wiped her eyes and laughed again, and Mary and Carl laughed.

After a time Carl unscrewed the top of the water pipe and blew through one of the tubes. "It gets plugged sometimes."

"What did you mean when you said I was on a bummer?" Jack said to Mary.

"What?" Mary said.

Jack stared at her and blinked. "You said something about me being on a bummer. What made you say that?"

"I don't remember now, but I can tell when you are," she said. "But please don't bring up anything negative, okay?"

"Okay," Jack said. "All I'm saying is I don't know why you said that. If I wasn't on a bummer before you said it, it's enough when you say it to put me on one."

"If the shoe fits," Mary said. She leaned on the arm of the sofa and laughed until tears came.

"What was that?" Carl said. He looked at Jack and then at Mary. "I missed that one," Carl said.

"I should have made some dip for these chips," Helen said.

"Wasn't there another bottle of that cream soda?" Carl said.

"We bought two bottles," Jack said.

"Did we drink them both?" Carl said.

"Did we drink any?" Helen said and laughed. "No, I only opened one. I think I only opened one. I don't remember opening more than one," Helen said and laughed.

Jack passed the tube to Mary. She took his hand and guided the tube into her mouth. He watched the smoke flow over her lips a long time later.

"What about some cream soda?" Carl said.

Mary and Helen laughed.

"What about it?" Mary said.

"Well, I thought we were going to have us a glass," Carl said. He looked at Mary and grinned.

Mary and Helen laughed.

"What's funny?" Carl said. He looked at Helen and then at Mary. He shook his head. "I don't know about you guys," he said.

"We might go to Alaska," Jack said.

"Alaska?" Carl said. "What's in Alaska? What would you do up there?"

"I wish we could go someplace," Helen said.

"What's wrong with here?" Carl said. "What would you guys do in Alaska? I'm serious. I'd like to know."

Jack put a potato chip in his mouth and sipped his cream soda. "I don't know. What did you say?"

After a while Carl said, "What's in Alaska?"

"I don't know," Jack said. "Ask Mary. Mary knows. Mary, what am I going to do up there? Maybe I'll grow those giant cabbages you read about."

"Or pumpkins," Helen said. "Grow pumpkins."

"You'd clean up," Carl said. "Ship the pumpkins down here for Hallowe'en. I'll be your distributor."

"Carl will be your distributor," Helen said.

"That's right," Carl said. "We'll clean up."

"Get rich," Mary said.

In a while Carl stood up. "I know what would taste good and that's some cream soda," Carl said.

Mary and Helen laughed.

"Go ahead and laugh," Carl said, grinning. "Who wants some?"

"Some what?" Mary said.

"Some cream soda," Carl said.

"You stood up like you were going to make a speech," Mary said.

"I hadn't thought of that," Carl said. He shook his head and laughed. He sat down. "That's good stuff," he said.

"We should have got more," Helen said.

"More what?" Mary said.

"More money," Carl said.

"No money," Jack said.

"Did I see some U-No bars in that sack?" Helen said.

"I bought some," Jack said. "I spotted them the last minute."

"U-No bars are good," Carl said.

"They're creamy," Mary said. "They melt in your mouth."

"We have some M&Ms and Popsicles if anybody wants any," Carl said.

Mary said, "I'll have a Popsicle. Are you going to the kitchen?"

"Yeah, and I'm going to get the cream soda, too," Carl said. "I just remembered. You guys want a glass?"

"Just bring it all in and we'll decide," Helen said. "The M&Ms too."

"Might be easier to move the kitchen out here," Carl said.

"When we lived in the city," Mary said, "people said you could see who'd turned on the night before by looking at their kitchen in the morning. We had a tiny kitchen when we lived in the city," she said.

"We had a tiny kitchen too," Jack said.

"I'm going out to see what I can find," Carl said.

"I'll come with you," Mary said.

Jack watched them walk to the kitchen. He settled back against the cushion and watched them walk. Then he leaned forward very slowly. He squinted. He saw Carl reach up to a shelf in the cupboard. He saw Mary move against Carl from behind and put her arms around his waist.

"Are you guys serious?" Helen said.

"Very serious," Jack said.

"About Alaska," Helen said.

He stared at her.

"I thought you said something," Helen said.

Carl and Mary came back. Carl carried a large bag of M&Ms and a bottle of cream soda. Mary sucked on an orange Popsicle.

"Anybody want a sandwich?" Helen said. "We have sandwich stuff."

"Isn't it funny," Mary said. "You start with the desserts first and then you move on to the main course."

"It's funny," Jack said.

"Are you being sarcastic, honey?" Mary said.

"Who wants cream soda?" Carl said. "A round of cream soda coming up."

Jack held his glass out and Carl poured it full. Jack set the glass on the coffee table, but in reaching for it he knocked over the glass and the soda poured onto his shoe.

"Goddamn it," Jack said. "How do you like that? I spilled it on my shoe."

"Helen, do we have a towel? Get Jack a towel," Carl said.

"Those were new shoes," Mary said. "He just got them."

"They look comfortable," Helen said a long time later and handed Jack a towel.

"That's what I told him," Mary said.

Jack took the shoe off and rubbed the leather with the towel.

"It's done for," he said. "That cream soda will never come out."

Mary and Carl and Helen laughed.

"That reminds me, I read something in the paper," Helen said. She pushed on the tip of her nose with a finger and narrowed her eyes. "I can't remember what it was now," she said.

Jack worked the shoe back on. He put both feet under the lamp and looked at the shoes together.

"What did you read?" Carl said.

"What?" Helen said.

"You said you read something in the paper," Carl said.

Helen laughed. "I was just thinking about Alaska, and I remembered them finding a prehistoric man in a block of ice. Something reminded me."

"That wasn't in Alaska," Carl said.

"Maybe it wasn't, but it reminded me of it," Helen said.

"What *about* Alaska, you guys?" Carl said.

"There's nothing in Alaska," Jack said.

"He's on a bummer," Mary said.

"What'll you guys *do* in Alaska?" Carl said.

"There's nothing to do in Alaska," Jack said. He put his feet under the coffee table. Then he moved them out under the light once more. "Who wants a new pair of shoes?" Jack said.

"What's that noise?" Helen said.

They listened. Something scratched at the door.

"It sounds like Cindy," Carl said. "I'd better let her in."

"While you're up, get me a Popsicle," Helen said. She put her head back and laughed.

"I'll have another one too, honey," Mary said. "What did I say? I mean *Carl*," Mary said. "Excuse me. I thought I was talking to Jack."

"Popsicles all around," Carl said. "You want a Popsicle, Jack?"

"What?"

"You want an orange Popsicle?"

"An orange one," Jack said.

"Four Popsicles coming up," Carl said.

In a while he came back with the Popsicles and handed them around. He sat down and they heard the scratching again.

"I knew I was forgetting something," Carl said. He got up and opened the front door.

"Good Christ," he said, "if this isn't something. I guess Cindy went out for dinner tonight. Hey, you guys, look at this."

The cat carried a mouse into the living room, stopped to look at them, then carried the mouse down the hall.

"Did you see what I just saw?" Mary said. "Talk about a bummer."

Carl turned the hall light on. The cat carried the mouse out of the hall and into the bathroom.

"She's eating this mouse," Carl said.

"I don't think I want her eating a mouse in my bathroom," Helen said. "Make her get out of there. Some of the children's things are in there."

"She's not going to get out of here," Carl said.

"What about the mouse?" Mary said.

"What the hell," Carl said. "Cindy's got to learn to hunt if we're going to Alaska."

"Alaska?" Helen said. "What's all this about Alaska?"

"Don't ask me," Carl said. He stood near the bathroom door and watched the cat. "Mary and Jack said they're going to Alaska. Cindy's got to learn to hunt."

Mary put her chin in her hands and stared into the hall.

"She's eating the mouse," Carl said.

Helen finished the last of the corn chips. "I told him I didn't want Cindy eating a mouse in the bathroom. Carl?" Helen said.

"What?"

"Make her get out of the bathroom, I said," Helen said.

"For Christ's sake," Carl said.

"Look," Mary said. "Ugh. The goddamn cat is coming in here," Mary said.

"What's she doing?" Jack said.

The cat dragged the mouse under the coffee table. She lay down under the table and licked the mouse. She held the mouse in her paws and licked slowly, from head to tail.

"The cat's high," Carl said.

"It gives you the shivers," Mary said.

"It's just nature," Carl said.

"Look at her eyes," Mary said. "Look at the way she looks at us. She's high, all right."

Carl came over to the sofa and sat beside Mary. Mary inched toward Jack to give Carl room. She rested her hand on Jack's knee.

They watched the cat eat the mouse.

"Don't you ever feed that cat?" Mary said to Helen.

Helen laughed.

"You guys ready for another smoke?" Carl said.

"We have to go," Jack said.

"What's your hurry?" Carl said.

"Stay a little longer," Helen said. "You don't have to go yet."

Jack stared at Mary, who was staring at Carl. Carl stared at something on the rug near his feet.

Helen picked through the M&Ms in her hand.

"I like the green ones best," Helen said.

"I have to work in the morning," Jack said.

"What a bummer he's on," Mary said. "You want to hear a bummer, folks? *There's* a bummer."

"Are you coming?" Jack said.

"Anybody want a glass of milk?" Carl said. "We've got some milk out there."

"I'm too full of cream soda," Mary said.

"There's no more cream soda," Carl said.

Helen laughed. She closed her eyes and then opened them and then laughed again.

"We have to go home," Jack said. In a while he stood up and said, "Did we have coats? I don't think we had coats."

"What? I don't think we had coats," Mary said. She stayed seated.

"We'd better go," Jack said.

"They have to go," Helen said.

Jack put his hands under Mary's shoulders and pulled her up.

"Goodbye, you guys," Mary said. She embraced Jack. "I'm so full I can hardly move," Mary said.

Helen laughed.

"Helen's always finding something to laugh at," Carl said, and Carl grinned. "What are you laughing at, Helen?"

"I don't know. Something Mary said," Helen said.

"What did I say?" Mary said.

"I can't remember," Helen said.

"We have to go," Jack said.

"So long," Carl said. "Take it easy."

Mary tried to laugh.

"Let's go," Jack said.

"Night, everybody," Carl said. "Night, Jack," Jack heard Carl say very, very slowly.

Outside, Mary held Jack's arm and walked with her head down. They moved slowly on the sidewalk. He listened to the scuffing sounds her shoes made. He heard the sharp and separate sound of a dog barking and above that a murmuring of very distant traffic.

She raised her head. "When we get home, Jack, I want to be fucked, talked to, diverted. Divert me, Jack. I need to be diverted tonight." She tightened her hold on his arm.

He could feel the dampness in that shoe. He unlocked the door and flipped the light.

"Come to bed," she said.

"I'm coming," he said.

He went to the kitchen and drank two glasses of water. He turned off the living-room light and felt his way along the wall into the bedroom.

"Jack!" she yelled. "Jack!"

"Jesus Christ, it's me!" he said. "I'm trying to get the light on."

He found the lamp, and she sat up in bed. Her eyes were bright. He pulled the stem on the alarm and began taking off his clothes. His knees trembled.

"Is there anything else to smoke?" she said.

"We don't have anything," he said.

"Then fix me a drink. We have something to drink. Don't tell me we don't have something to drink," she said.

"Just some beer."

They stared at each other.

"I'll have a beer," she said.

"You really want a beer?"

She nodded slowly and chewed her lip.

He came back with the beer. She was sitting with his pillow on her lap. He gave her the can of beer and then crawled into bed and pulled the covers up.

"I forgot to take my pill," she said.

"What?"

"I forgot my pill."

He got out of bed and brought her the pill. She opened her eyes and he dropped the pill onto her outstretched tongue. She swallowed some beer with the pill and he got back in bed.

"Take this. I can't keep my eyes open," she said.

He set the can on the floor and then stayed on his side and stared into the dark hallway. She put her arm over his ribs and her fingers crept across his chest.

"What's in Alaska?" she said.

He turned on his stomach and eased all the way to his side of the bed. In a moment she was snoring.

Just as he started to turn off the lamp, he thought he saw something in the hall. He kept staring and thought he saw it again, a pair of small eyes. His heart turned. He blinked and kept staring. He leaned over to look for something to throw. He picked up one of his shoes. He sat up straight and held the shoe with both hands. He heard her snoring and set his teeth. He waited. He waited for it to move once more, to make the slightest noise.

Night School

My marriage had just fallen apart. I couldn't find a job. I had another girl. But she wasn't in town. So I was at a bar having a glass of beer, and two women were sitting a few stools down, and one of them began to talk to me.

"You have a car?"

"I do, but it's not here," I said.

My wife had the car. I was staying at my parents' place. I used their car sometimes. But tonight I was walking.

The other woman looked at me. They were both about forty, maybe older.

"What'd you ask him?" the other woman said to the first woman.

"I said did he have a car."

"So do you have a car?" the second woman said to me.

"I was telling her. I have a car. But I don't have it with me," I said.

"That doesn't do us much good, does it?" she said.

The first woman laughed. "We had a brainstorm and we need a car to go through with it. Too bad." She turned to the bartender and asked for two more beers.

I'd been nursing my beer along, and now I drank it off and thought they might buy me a round. They didn't.

"What do you do?" the first woman asked me.

"Right now, nothing," I said. "Sometimes, when I can, I go to school."

"He goes to school," she said to the other woman. "He's a student. Where do you go to school?"

"Around," I said.

"I told you," the woman said. "Doesn't he look like a student?"

"What are they teaching you?" the second woman said.

"Everything," I said.

"I mean," she said, "what do you plan to do? What's your big goal in life? Everybody has a big goal in life."

I raised my empty glass to the bartender. He took it and drew me another beer. I counted out some change, which left me with thirty cents from the two dollars I'd started out with a couple of hours ago. She was waiting.

"Teach. Teach school," I said.

"He wants to be a teacher," she said.

I sipped my beer. Someone put a coin in the jukebox and a song that my wife liked began to play. I looked around. Two men near the front were at the shuffleboard. The door was open and it was dark outside.

"We're students too, you know," the first woman said. "We go to school."

"We take a night class," the other one said. "We take this reading class on Monday nights."

The first woman said, "Why don't you move down here, teacher, so we don't have to yell?"

I picked up my beer and my cigarettes and moved down two stools.

"That's better," she said. "Now, did you say you were a student?"

"Sometimes, yes, but not now," I said.

"Where?"

"State College."

"That's right," she said. "I remember now." She looked at the other woman. "You ever hear of a teacher over there name of Patterson? He teaches adult education classes. He teaches this class we take on Monday nights. You remind me a lot of Patterson."

They looked at each other and laughed.

"Don't bother about us," the first woman said. "It's a private joke. Shall we tell him what we thought about doing, Edith? *Shall* we?"

Edith didn't answer. She took a drink of beer and she narrowed her eyes as she looked at herself, at the three of us, in the mirror behind the bar.

"We were thinking," the first woman went on, "if we had a car tonight we'd go over and see him. Patterson. Right, Edith?"

Edith laughed to herself. She finished her beer and asked for a round, one for me included. She paid for the beers with a five-dollar bill.

"Patterson likes to take a drink," Edith said.

"You can say that again," the other woman said. She turned to me. "We

71

talked about it in class one night. Patterson says he always has wine with his meals and a highball or two before dinner."

"What class is this?" I said.

"This reading class Patterson teaches. Patterson likes to talk about different things."

"We're learning to read," Edith said. "Can you believe it?"

"I'd like to read Hemingway and things like that," the other woman said. "But Patterson has us reading stories like in *Reader's Digest*."

"We take a test every Monday night," Edith said. "But Patterson's okay. He wouldn't care if we came over for a highball. Wouldn't be much he could do, anyway. We have something on him. On Patterson," she said.

"We're on the loose tonight," the other woman said. "But Edith's car is in the garage."

"If you had a car now, we'd go over and see him," Edith said. She looked at me. "You could tell Patterson you wanted to be a teacher. You'd have something in common."

I finished my beer. I hadn't eaten anything all day except some peanuts. It was hard to keep listening and talking.

"Let's have three more, please, Jerry," the first woman said to the bartender.

"Thank you," I said.

"You'd get along with Patterson," Edith said.

"So call him," I said. I thought it was just talk.

"I wouldn't do that," she said. "He could make an excuse. We just show up on his porch, he'll have to let us in." She sipped her beer.

"So let's go!" the first woman said. "What're we waiting for? Where'd you say the car is?"

"There's a car a few blocks from here," I said. "But I don't know."

"Do you want to go or don't you?" Edith said.

"He said he does," the first woman said. "We'll get a six-pack to take with us."

"I only have thirty cents," I said.

"Who needs your goddamn money?" Edith said. "We need your goddamn car. Jerry, let's have three more. And a six-pack to go."

"Here's to Patterson," the first woman said when the beer came. "To Patterson and his highballs."

"He'll drop his cookies," Edith said.

"Drink up," the first woman said.

On the sidewalk we headed south, away from town. I walked between the two women. It was about ten o'clock.

"I could drink one of those beers now," I said.

"Help yourself," Edith said.

She opened the sack and I reached in and tore a can loose.

"We think he's home," Edith said.

"Patterson," the other woman said. "We don't know for sure. But we think so."

"How much farther?" Edith said.

I stopped, raised the beer, and drained half the can. "The next block," I said. "I'm staying with my parents. It's their place."

"I guess there's nothing wrong with it," Edith said. "But I'd say you're kind of old for that."

"That's not polite, Edith," the other woman said.

"Well, that's the way I am," Edith said. "He'll have to get used to it, that's all. That's the way I am."

"That's the way she is," the other woman said.

I finished the beer and tossed the can into some weeds.

"Now how far?" Edith said.

"This is it. Right here. I'll try and get the car key," I said.

"Well, hurry up," Edith said.

"We'll wait outside," the other woman said.

"Jesus!" Edith said.

I unlocked the door and went downstairs. My father was in his pajamas, watching television. It was warm in the apartment and I leaned against the jamb for a minute and ran a hand over my eyes.

"I had a couple of beers," I said. "What are you watching?"

"John Wayne," he said. "It's pretty good. Sit down and watch it. Your mother hasn't come in yet."

My mother worked the swing shift at Paul's, a *hofbrau* restaurant. My father didn't have a job. He used to work in the woods, and then he got hurt. He'd had a settlement, but most of that was gone now. I asked him for a loan of two hundred dollars when my wife left me, but he refused. He had tears in his eyes when he said no and said he hoped I wouldn't hold it against him. I'd said it was all right, I wouldn't hold it against him.

I knew he was going to say no this time too. But I sat down on the other end of the couch and said, "I met a couple of women who asked me if I'd give them a ride home."

"What'd you tell them?" he said.

"They're waiting for me upstairs," I said.

"Just let them wait," he said. "Somebody'll come along. You don't want to get mixed up with that." He shook his head. "You really didn't show them where we live, did you? They're not really upstairs?" He moved on the couch and looked again at the television. "Anyway, your mother took the keys with her." He nodded slowly, still looking at the television.

"That's okay," I said. "I don't need the car. I'm not going anywhere."

I got up and looked into the hallway, where I slept on a cot. There was an ashtray, a Lux clock, and a few old paperbacks on a table beside the cot. I usually went to bed at midnight and read until the lines of print went fuzzy and I fell asleep with the light on and the book in my hands. In one of the paperbacks I was reading there was something I remembered telling my wife. It made a terrific impression on me. There's a man who has a nightmare and in the nightmare he dreams he's dreaming and wakes to see a man standing at his bedroom window. The dreamer is so terrified he can't move, can hardly breathe. The man at the window stares into the room and then begins to pry off the screen. The dreamer can't move. He'd like to scream, but he can't get his breath. But the moon appears from behind a cloud, and the dreamer in the nightmare recognizes the man outside. It is his best friend, the best friend of the dreamer but no one the man having the nightmare knows.

Telling it to my wife, I'd felt the blood come to my face and my scalp prickle. But she wasn't interested.

"That's only writing," she said. "Being betrayed by somebody in your own family, *there's* a real nightmare for you."

I could hear them shaking the outside door. I could hear footsteps on the sidewalk over my window.

"Goddamn that bastard!" I heard Edith say.

I went into the bathroom for a long time and then I went upstairs and let myself out. It was cooler, and I did up the zipper on my jacket. I started walking to Paul's. If I got there before my mother went off duty, I could have a turkey sandwich. After that I could go to Kirby's newsstand and look through the magazines. Then I could go to the apartment to bed and read the books until I read enough and I slept.

The women, they weren't there when I left, and they wouldn't be there when I got back.

Collectors

I was out of work. But any day I expected to hear from up north. I lay on the sofa and listened to the rain. Now and then I'd lift up and look through the curtain for the mailman.

There was no one on the street, nothing.

I hadn't been down again five minutes when I heard someone walk onto the porch, wait, and then knock. I lay still. I knew it wasn't the mailman. I knew his steps. You can't be too careful if you're out of work and you get notices in the mail or else pushed under your door. They come around wanting to talk, too, especially if you don't have a telephone.

The knock sounded again, louder, a bad sign. I eased up and tried to see onto the porch. But whoever was there was standing against the door, another bad sign. I knew the floor creaked, so there was no chance of slipping into the other room and looking out that window.

Another knock, and I said, Who's there?

This is Aubrey Bell, a man said. Are you Mr Slater?

What is it you want? I called from the sofa.

I have something for Mrs Slater. She's won something. Is Mrs Slater home?

Mrs Slater doesn't live here, I said.

Well, then, are you Mr Slater? the man said. Mr Slater . . . and the man sneezed.

I got off the sofa. I unlocked the door and opened it a little. He was an old guy, fat and bulky under his raincoat. Water ran off the coat and dripped onto the big suitcase contraption thing he carried.

He grinned and set down the big case. He put out his hand.

Aubrey Bell, he said.

I don't know you, I said.

Mrs Slater, he began. Mrs Slater filled out a card. He took cards from an inside pocket and shuffled them a minute. Mrs Slater, he read. Two-fifty-five South Sixth East? Mrs Slater is a winner.

He took off his hat and nodded solemnly, slapped the hat against his coat as if that were it, everything had been settled, the drive finished, the railhead reached.

He waited.

Mrs Slater doesn't live here, I said. What'd she win?

I have to show you, he said. May I come in?

I don't know. If it won't take long, I said. I'm pretty busy.

Fine, he said. I'll just slide out of this coat first. And the galoshes. Wouldn't want to track up your carpet. I see you do have a carpet, Mr . . .

His eyes had lighted and then dimmed at the sight of the carpet. He shuddered. Then he took off his coat. He shook it out and hung it by the collar over the doorknob. That's a good place for it, he said. Damn weather, anyway. He bent over and unfastened his galoshes. He set his case inside the room. He stepped out of the galoshes and into the room in a pair of slippers.

I closed the door. He saw me staring at the slippers and said, W. H. Auden wore slippers all through China on his first visit there. Never took them off. Corns.

I shrugged. I took one more look down the street for the mailman and shut the door again.

Aubrey Bell stared at the carpet. He pulled his lips. Then he laughed. He laughed and shook his head.

What's so funny? I said.

Nothing. Lord, he said. He laughed again. I think I'm losing my mind. I think I have a fever. He reached a hand to his forehead. His hair was matted and there was a ring around his scalp where the hat had been.

Do I feel hot to you? he said. I don't know, I think I might have a fever. He was still staring at the carpet. You have any aspirin?

What's the matter with you? I said. I hope you're not getting sick on me. I got things I have to do.

He shook his head. He sat down on the sofa. He stirred at the carpet with his slippered foot.

I went to the kitchen, rinsed a cup, shook two aspirin out of a bottle. Here, I said. Then I think you ought to leave.

Are you speaking for Mrs Slater? he hissed. No, no, forget I said that, forget I said that. He wiped his face. He swallowed the aspirin. His eyes skipped around the bare room. Then he leaned forward with some effort and unsnapped the buckles on his case. The case flopped open, revealing compartments filled with an array of hoses, brushes, shiny pipes, and some kind of heavy-looking blue thing mounted on little wheels. He stared at these things as if surprised. Quietly, in a churchly voice, he said, Do you know what this is?

I moved closer. I'd say it was a vacuum cleaner. I'm not in the market, I said. No way am I in the market for a vacuum cleaner.

I want to show you something, he said. He took a card out of his jacket pocket. Look at this, he said. He handed me the card. Nobody said you were in the market. But look at the signature. Is that Mrs Slater's signature or not?

I looked at the card. I held it up to the light. I turned it over, but the other side was blank. So what? I said.

Mrs Slater's card was pulled at random out of a basket of cards. Hundreds of cards just like this little card. She has won a free vacuuming and carpet shampoo. Mrs Slater is a winner. No strings. I am here even to do your mattress, Mr . . . You'll be surprised to see what can collect in a mattress over the months, over the years. Every day, every night of our lives, we're leaving little bits of ourselves, flakes of this and that, behind. Where do they go, these bits and pieces of ourselves? Right through the sheets and into the mattress, *that's* where! Pillows, too. It's all the same.

He had been removing lengths of the shiny pipe and joining the parts together. Now he inserted the fitted pipes into the hose. He was on his knees, grunting. He attached some sort of scoop to the hose and lifted out the blue thing with wheels.

He let me examine the filter he intended to use.

Do you have a car? he asked.

No car, I said. I don't have a car. If I had a car I would drive you someplace.

Too bad, he said. This little vacuum comes equipped with a sixty-foot extension cord. If you had a car, you could wheel this little vacuum right up to your car door and vacuum the plush carpeting and the luxurious reclining seats as well. You would be surprised how much of us gets lost, how much of us gathers, in those fine seats over the years.

Mr Bell, I said, I think you better pack up your things and go. I say this without any malice whatsoever.

But he was looking around the room for a plug-in. He found one at the end of the sofa. The machine rattled as if there were a marble inside, anyway something loose inside, then settled to a hum.

Rilke lived in one castle after another, all of his adult life. Benefactors, he said loudly over the hum of the vacuum. He seldom rode in motorcars; he preferred trains. Then look at Voltaire at Cirey with Madame Châtelet. His death mask. Such serenity. He raised his right hand as if I were about to disagree. No, no, it isn't right, is it? Don't say it. But who knows? With that he turned and began to pull the vacuum into the other room.

There was a bed, a window. The covers were heaped on the floor. One pillow, one sheet over the mattress. He slipped the case from the pillow and then quickly stripped the sheet from the mattress. He stared at the mattress and gave me a look out of the corner of his eye. I went to the kitchen and got the chair. I sat down in the doorway and watched. First he tested the suction by putting the scoop against the palm of his hand. He bent and turned a dial on the vacuum. You have to turn it up full strength for a job like this one, he said. He checked the suction again, then extended the hose to the head of the bed and began to move the scoop down the mattress. The scoop tugged at the mattress. The vacuum whirred louder. He made three passes over the mattress, then switched off the machine. He pressed a lever and the lid popped open. He took out the filter. This filter is just for demonstration purposes. In normal use, all of this, this *material*, would go into your bag, here, he said. He pinched some of the dusty stuff between his fingers. There must have been a cup of it.

He had this look to his face.

It's not my mattress, I said. I leaned forward in the chair and tried to show an interest.

Now the pillow, he said. He put the used filter on the sill and looked out the window for a minute. He turned. I want you to hold onto this end of the pillow, he said.

I got up and took hold of two corners of the pillow. I felt I was holding something by the ears.

Like this? I said.

He nodded. He went into the other room and came back with another filter.

How much do those things cost? I said.

Next to nothing, he said. They're only made out of paper and a little bit of plastic. Couldn't cost much.

He kicked on the vacuum and I held tight as the scoop sank into the pillow and moved down its length – once, twice, three times. He switched off the vacuum, removed the filter, and held it up without a word. He put it on the sill beside the other filter. Then he opened the closet door. He looked inside, but there was only a box of Mouse-Be-Gone.

I heard steps on the porch, the mail slot opened and clinked shut. We looked at each other.

He pulled on the vacuum and I followed him into the other room. We looked at the letter lying face down on the carpet near the front door.

I started toward the letter, turned and said, What else? It's getting late. This carpet's not worth fooling with. It's only a twelve-by-fifteen cotton carpet with no-skid backing from Rug City. It's not worth fooling with.

Do you have a full ashtray? he said. Or a potted plant or something like that? A handful of dirt would be fine.

I found the ashtray. He took it, dumped the contents onto the carpet, ground the ashes and cigarettes under his slipper. He got down on his knees again and inserted a new filter. He took off his jacket and threw it onto the sofa. He was sweating under the arms. Fat hung over his belt. He twisted off the scoop and attached another device to the hose. He adjusted his dial. He kicked on the machine and began to move back and forth, back and forth over the worn carpet. Twice I started for the letter. But he seemed to anticipate me, cut me off, so to speak, with his hose and his pipes and his sweeping and his sweeping. . .

I took the chair back to the kitchen and sat there and watched him work. After a time he shut off the machine, opened the lid, and silently brought me the filter, alive with dust, hair, small grainy things. I looked at the filter, and then I got up and put it in the garbage.

He worked steadily now. No more explanations. He came out to the kitchen with a bottle that held a few ounces of green liquid. He put the bottle under the tap and filled it.

You know I can't pay anything, I said. I couldn't pay you a dollar if my life depended on it. You're going to have to write me off as a dead loss, that's all. You're wasting your time on me, I said.

I wanted it out in the open, no misunderstanding.

He went about his business. He put another attachment on the hose, in some complicated way hooked his bottle to the new attachment. He moved slowly over the carpet, now and then releasing little streams of emerald, moving the brush back and forth over the carpet, working up patches of foam.

I had said all that was on my mind. I sat on the chair in the kitchen, relaxed now, and watched him work. Once in a while I looked out the window at the rain. It had begun to get dark. He switched off the vacuum. He was in a corner near the front door.

You want coffee? I said.

He was breathing hard. He wiped his face.

I put on water and by the time it had boiled and I'd fixed up two cups he had everything dismantled and back in the case. Then he picked up the letter. He read the name on the letter and looked closely at the return address. He folded the letter in half and put it in his hip pocket. I kept watching him. That's all I did. The coffee began to cool.

It's for a Mr Slater, he said. I'll see to it. He said, Maybe I will skip the coffee. I better not walk across this carpet. I just shampooed it.

That's true, I said. Then I said, You're sure that's who the letter's for?

He reached to the sofa for his jacket, put it on, and opened the front door. It was still raining. He stepped into his galoshes, fastened them, and then pulled on the raincoat and looked back inside.

You want to see it? he said. You don't believe me?

It just seems strange, I said.

Well, I'd better be off, he said. But he kept standing there. You want the vacuum or not?

I looked at the big case, closed now and ready to move on.

No, I said, I guess not. I'm going to be leaving here soon. It would just be in the way.

All right, he said, and he shut the door.

What Do You Do in San Francisco?

This has nothing to do with me. It's about a young couple with three children who moved into a house on my route the first of last summer. I got to thinking about them again when I picked up last Sunday's newspaper and found a picture of a young man who'd been arrested down in San Francisco for killing his wife and her boyfriend with a baseball bat. It wasn't the same man, of course, though there was a likeness because of the beard. But the situation was close enough to get me thinking.

Henry Robinson is the name. I'm a postman, a federal civil servant, and have been since 1947. I've lived in the West all my life, except for a three-year stint in the Army during the war. I've been divorced twenty years, have two children I haven't seen in almost that long. I'm not a frivolous man, nor am I, in my opinion, a serious man. It's my belief a man has to be a little of both these days. I believe, too, in the value of work – the harder the better. A man who isn't working has got too much time on his hands, too much time to dwell on himself and his problems.

I'm convinced that was partly the trouble with the young man who lived here – his not working. But I'd lay that at her doorstep, too. The woman. She encouraged it.

Beatniks, I guess you'd have called them if you'd seen them. The man wore a pointed brown beard on his chin and looked like he needed to sit down to a good dinner and a cigar afterward. The woman was attractive, with her long dark hair and her fair complexion, there's no getting around that. But put me down for saying she wasn't a good wife and mother. She was a painter. The young man, I don't know what he did – probably something along the same line. Neither of them worked. But they paid their rent and got by somehow – at least for the summer.

The first time I saw them it was around eleven, eleven-fifteen, a Saturday morning. I was about two-thirds through my route when I turned onto their block and noticed a '56 Ford sedan pulled up in the yard with a big open U-Haul behind. There are only three houses on Pine, and theirs was the last house, the others being the Murchisons, who'd been in Arcata a little less than a year, and the Grants, who'd been here about two years. Murchison worked at Simpson Redwood, and Gene Grant was a cook on the morning shift at Denny's. Those two, then a vacant lot, then the house on the end that used to belong to the Coles.

The young man was out in the yard behind the trailer and she was just coming out the front door with a cigarette in her mouth, wearing a tight pair of white jeans and a man's white undershirt. She stopped when she saw me and she stood watching me come down the walk. I slowed up when I came even with their box and nodded in her direction.

"Getting settled all right?" I asked.

"It'll be a little while," she said and moved a handful of hair away from her forehead while she continued to smoke.

"That's good," I said. "Welcome to Arcata."

I felt a little awkward after saying it. I don't know why, but I always found myself feeling awkward the few times I was around this woman. It was one of the things helped turn me against her from the first.

She gave me a thin smile and I started to move on when the young man – Marston was his name – came around from behind the trailer carrying a big carton of toys. Now, Arcata is not a small town and it's not a big town, though I guess you'd have to say it's more on the small side. It's not the end of the world, Arcata, by any means, but most of the people who live here work either in the lumber mills or have something to do with the fishing industry, or else work in one of the downtown stores. People here aren't used to seeing men wear beards – or men who don't work, for that matter.

"Hello," I said. I put out my hand when he set the carton down on the front fender. "The name's Henry Robinson. You folks just arrive?"

"Yesterday afternoon," he said.

"Some trip! It took us fourteen hours just to come from San Francisco," the woman spoke up from the porch. "Pulling that damn trailer."

"My, my," I said and shook my head. "San Francisco? I was just down in San Francisco, let me see, last April or March."

"You were, were you?" she said. "What did you do in San Francisco?"

"Oh, nothing, really. I go down about once or twice a year. Out to Fisherman's Wharf and to see the Giants play. That's about all."

There was a little pause and Marston examined something in the grass with his toe. I started to move on. The kids picked that moment to come flying out the front door, yelling and tearing for the end of the porch. When that screen door banged open, I thought Marston was going to jump out of his skin. But she just stood there with her arms crossed, cool as a cucumber, and never batted an eye. He didn't look good at all. Quick, jerky little movements every time he made to do something. And his eyes – they'd land on you and then slip off somewheres else, then land on you again.

There were three kids, two little curly-headed girls about four or five, and a little bit of a boy tagging after.

"Cute kids," I said. "Well, I got to get under way. You might want to change the name on the box."

"Sure," he said. "Sure. I'll see about it in a day or two. But we don't expect to get any mail for a while yet, in any case."

"You never know," I said. "You never know what'll turn up in this old mail pouch. Wouldn't hurt to be prepared." I started to go. "By the way, if you're looking for a job in the mills, I can tell you who to see at Simpson Redwood. A friend of mine's a foreman there. He'd probably have something . . ." I tapered off, seeing how they didn't look interested.

"No, thanks," he said.

"He's not looking for a job," she put in.

"Well, goodbye, then."

"So long," Marston said.

Not another word from her.

That was on a Saturday, as I said, the day before Memorial Day. We took Monday as a holiday and I wasn't by there again until Tuesday. I can't say I was surprised to see the U-Haul still there in the front yard. But it did surprise me to see he still hadn't unloaded it. I'd say about a quarter of the stuff had made its way to the front porch – a covered chair and a chrome kitchen chair and a big carton of clothes that had the flaps pulled off the top. Another quarter must have gotten inside the house, and the rest of the stuff was still in the trailer. The kids were carrying little sticks and hammering on the sides of the trailer as they climbed in and out over the tailgate. Their mamma and daddy were nowheres to be seen.

On Thursday I saw him out in the yard again and reminded him about changing the name on the box.

"That's something I've got to get around to doing," he said.

"Takes time," I said. "There's lots of things to take care of when you're moving into a new place. People that lived here, the Coles, just moved out two days before you came. He was going to work in Eureka. With the Fish and Game Department."

Marston stroked his beard and looked off as if thinking of something else.

"I'll be seeing you," I said.

"So long," he said.

Well, the long and the short of it was he never did change the name on the box. I'd come along a bit later with a piece of mail for that address and he'd say something like, "Marston? Yes, that's for us, Marston. . . I'll have to change the name on that box one of these days. I'll get myself a can of paint and just paint over that other name . . . Cole," all the time his eyes drifting here and there. Then he'd look at me kind of out the corners and bob his chin once or twice. But he never did change the name on the box, and after a time I shrugged and forgot about it.

You hear rumors. At different times I heard that he was an ex-con on parole who come to Arcata to get out of the unhealthy San Francisco environment. According to this story, the woman was his wife, but none of the kids belonged to him. Another story was that he had committed a crime and was hiding out here. But not many people subscribed to that. He just didn't look the sort who'd do something really *criminal*. The story most folks seemed to believe, at least the one that got around most, was the most horrible. The woman was a dope addict, so this story went, and the husband had brought her up here to help her get rid of the habit. As evidence, the fact of Sallie Wilson's visit was always brought up – Sallie Wilson from the Welcome Wagon. She dropped in on them one afternoon and said later that, no lie, there was something funny about them – the woman, particular. One minute the woman would be sitting and listening to Sallie run on – all ears, it seemed – and the next she'd get up while Sallie was still talking and start to work on her painting as if Sallie wasn't there. Also the way she'd be fondling and kissing the kids, then suddenly start screeching at them for no apparent reason. Well, just the way her *eyes* looked if you came up close to her, Sallie said. But Sallie Wilson has been snooping and prying for years under cover of the Welcome Wagon.

"You don't know," I'd say when someone would bring it up. "Who can say? If he'd just go to work now."

All the same, the way it looked to me was that they had their fair share of trouble down there in San Francisco, whatever was the nature of the trouble, and they decided to get clear away from it. Though why they ever picked Arcata to settle in, it's hard to say, since they surely didn't come looking for work.

The first few weeks there was no mail to speak of, just a few circulars, from Sears and Western Auto and the like. Then a few letters began to come in, maybe one or two a week. Sometimes I'd see one or the other of them out around the house when I came by and sometimes not. But the kids were always there, running in and out of the house or playing in the vacant lot next door. Of course, it wasn't a model home to begin with, but after they'd been there a while the weeds sprouted up and what grass there was yellowed and died. You hate to see something like that. I understand Old Man Jessup came out once or twice to get them to turn the water on, but they claimed they couldn't buy a hose. So he left them a hose. Then I noticed the kids playing with it over in the field, and that was the end of that. Twice I saw a little white sports car in front, a car that hadn't come from around here.

One time only I had anything to do with the woman direct. There was a letter with postage due, and I went up to the door with it. One of the little girls let me in and ran off to fetch her mama. The place was cluttered with odds and ends of old furniture and with clothing tossed just anywhere. But it wasn't what you'd call dirty. Not tidy maybe, but not dirty either. An old couch and chair stood along one wall in the living room. Under the window was a bookcase made out of bricks and boards, crammed full of little paperback books. In the corner there was a stack of paintings with their faces turned away, and to one side another painting stood on an easel covered over with a sheet.

I shifted my mail pouch and stood my ground, but starting to wish I'd paid the difference myself. I eyed the easel as I waited, about to sidle over and raise the sheet when I heard steps.

"What can I do for you?" she said, appearing in the hallway and not at all friendly.

I touched the brim of my cap and said, "A letter here with postage due, if you don't mind."

"Let me see. Who's it from? Why it's from Jer! That kook. Sending us a letter without a stamp. Lee!" she called out. "Here's a letter from Jerry." Marston came in, but he didn't look too happy. I leaned on first one leg, then the other, waiting.

"I'll pay it," she said, "seeing as it's from old Jerry. Here. Now goodbye."

Things went on in this fashion – which is to say no fashion at all. I won't say the people hereabouts got used to them – they weren't the sort you'd ever really get used to. But after a bit no one seemed to pay them much mind any more. People might stare at his beard if they met him pushing the grocery cart in Safeway, but that's about all. You didn't hear any more stories.

Then one day they disappeared. In two different directions. I found out later she'd taken off the week before with somebody – a man – and that after a few days he'd taken the kids to his mother's over to Redding. For six days running, from one Thursday to the following Wednesday, their mail stayed in the box. The shades were all pulled and nobody knew for certain whether or not they'd lit out for good. But that Wednesday I noticed the Ford parked in the yard again, all the shades still down but the mail gone.

Beginning the next day he was out there at the box every day waiting for me to hand over the mail, or else he was sitting on the porch steps smoking a cigarette, waiting, it was plain to see. When he saw me coming, he'd stand up, brush the seat of his trousers, and walk over by the box. If it happened that I had any mail for him, I'd see him start scanning the return addresses even before I could get it handed over. We seldom exchanged a word, just nodded at each other if our eyes happened to meet, which wasn't often. He was suffering, though – anybody could see that – and I wanted to help the boy somehow, if I could. But I didn't know what to say exactly.

It was one morning a week or so after his return that I saw him walking up and down in front of the box with his hands in his back pockets, and I made up my mind to say something. What, I didn't know yet, but I was going to say something, sure. His back was to me as I came up the walk.

When I got to him, he suddenly turned on me and there was such a look on his face it froze the words in my mouth. I stopped in my tracks with his article of mail. He took a couple of steps toward me and I handed it over without a peep. He stared at it as if dumbfounded.

"Occupant," he said.

It was a circular from L.A. advertising a hospital-insurance plan. I'd dropped off at least seventy-five that morning. He folded it in two and went back to the house.

Next day he was out there same as always. He had his old look to his face, seemed more in control of himself than the day before. This time I had a hunch I had what it was he'd been waiting for. I'd looked at it down at the station that morning when I was arranging the mail into packets. It was a plain white envelope addressed in a woman's curlicue handwriting that took up most of the space. It had a Portland postmark, and the return address showed the initials J.D. and a Portland street address.

"Morning," I said, offering the letter.

He took it from me without a word and went absolutely pale. He tottered a minute and then started back for the house, holding the letter up to the light.

I called out, "She's no good, boy. I could tell that the minute I saw her. Why don't you forget her? Why don't you go to work and forget her? What have you got against work? It was work, day and night, work that gave me oblivion when I was in your shoes and there was a war on where I was. . ."

After that he didn't wait outside for me any more, and he was only there another five days. I'd catch a glimpse of him, though, each day, waiting for me just the same, but standing behind the window and looking out at me through the curtain. He wouldn't come out until I'd gone by, and then I'd hear the screen door. If I looked back, he'd seem to be in no hurry at all to reach the box.

The last time I saw him he was standing at the window and looked calm and rested. The curtains were down, all the shades were raised, and I figured at the time he was getting his things together to leave. But I could tell by the look on his face he wasn't watching for me this time. He was staring past me, over me, you might say, over the rooftops and the trees, south. He just kept staring even after I'd come even with the house and moved on down the sidewalk. I looked back. I could see him still there at the window. The feeling was so strong, I had to turn around and look for myself in the same direction he was. But, as you might guess, I didn't see anything except the same old timber, mountains, sky.

The next day he was gone. He didn't leave any forwarding. Sometimes mail of some kind or other shows up for him or his wife or for the both of them. If it's first-class, we hold it a day, then send it back to where it came from. There isn't much. And I don't mind. It's all work, one way or the other, and I'm always glad to have it.

The Student's Wife

He had been reading to her from Rilke, a poet he admired, when she fell asleep with her head on his pillow. He liked reading aloud, and he read well – a confident sonorous voice, now pitched low and somber, now rising, now thrilling. He never looked away from the page when he read and stopped only to reach to the nightstand for a cigarette. It was a rich voice that spilled her into a dream of caravans just setting out from walled cities and bearded men in robes. She had listened to him for a few minutes, then she had closed her eyes and drifted off.

He went on reading aloud. The children had been asleep for hours, and outside a car rubbered by now and then on the wet pavement. After a while he put down the book and turned in the bed to reach for the lamp. She opened her eyes suddenly, as if frightened, and blinked two or three times. Her eyelids looked oddly dark and fleshy to him as they flicked up and down over her fixed glassy eyes. He stared at her.

"Are you dreaming?" he asked.

She nodded and brought her hand up and touched her fingers to the plastic curlers at either side of her head. Tomorrow would be Friday, her day for all the four-to-seven-year-olds in the Woodlawn Apartments. He kept looking at her, leaning on his elbow, at the same time trying to straighten the spread with his free hand. She had a smooth-skinned face with prominent cheekbones; the cheekbones, she sometimes insisted to friends, were from her father, who had been one-quarter Nez Perce.

Then: "Make me a little sandwich of something, Mike. With butter and lettuce and salt on the bread."

He did nothing and he said nothing because he wanted to go to sleep. But when he opened his eyes she was still awake, watching him.

"Can't you go to sleep, Nan?" he said, very solemnly. "It's late."

"I'd like something to eat first," she said. "My legs and arms hurt for some reason, and I'm hungry."

He groaned extravagantly as he rolled out of bed.

He fixed her the sandwich and brought it in on a saucer. She sat up

in bed and smiled when he came into the bedroom, then slipped a
pillow behind her back as she took the saucer. He thought she looked
like a hospital patient in her white nightgown.

"What a funny little dream I had."

"What were you dreaming?" he said, getting into bed and turning over
onto his side away from her. He stared at the nightstand waiting. Then he
closed his eyes slowly.

"Do you really want to hear it?" she said.

"Sure," he said.

She settled back comfortably on the pillow and picked a crumb from
her lip.

"Well. It seemed like a real long drawn-out kind of dream, you know,
with all kinds of relationships going on, but I can't remember everything
now. It was all very clear when I woke up, but it's beginning to fade now.
How long have I been asleep, Mike? It doesn't really matter, I guess.
Anyway, I think it was that we were staying someplace overnight. I don't
know where the kids were, but it was just the two of us at some little hotel
or something. It was on some lake that wasn't familiar. There was another,
older, couple there and they wanted to take us for a ride in their motor-
boat." She laughed, remembering, and leaned forward off the pillow. "The
next thing I recall is we were down at the boat landing. Only the way it
turned out, they had just one seat in the boat, a kind of bench up in the
front, and it was only big enough for three. You and I started arguing about
who was going to sacrifice and sit all cooped up in the back. You said you
were, and I said I was. But I finally squeezed in the back of the boat. It
was so narrow it hurt my legs, and I was afraid the water was going to
come in over the sides. Then I woke up."

"That's some dream," he managed to say and felt drowsily that he should
say something more. "You remember Bonnie Travis? Fred Travis' wife?
She used to have *color* dreams, she said."

She looked at the sandwich in her hand and took a bite. When she had
swallowed, she ran her tongue in behind her lips and balanced the saucer
on her lap as she reached behind and plumped up the pillow. Then she
smiled and leaned back against the pillow again.

"Do you remember that time we stayed overnight on the Tilton River,
Mike? When you caught that big fish the next morning?" She placed her
hand on his shoulder. "Do you remember that?" she said.

She did. After scarcely thinking about it these last years, it had begun coming back to her lately. It was a month or two after they'd married and gone away for a weekend. They had sat by a little campfire that night, a watermelon in the snow-cold river, and she'd fried Spam and eggs and canned beans for supper and pancakes and Spam and eggs in the same blackened pan the next morning. She had burned the pan both times she cooked, and they could never get the coffee to boil, but it was one of the best times they'd ever had. She remembered he had read to her that night as well: Elizabeth Browning and a few poems from the *Rubáiyát*. They had had so many covers over them that she could hardly turn her feet under all the weight. The next morning he had hooked a big trout, and people stopped their cars on the road across the river to watch him play it in.

"Well? Do you remember or not?" she said, patting him on the shoulder. "Mike?"

"I remember," he said. He shifted a little on his side, opened his eyes. He did not remember very well, he thought. What he did remember was very carefully combed hair and loud half-baked ideas about life and art, and he did not want to remember that.

"That was a long time ago, Nan," he said.

"We'd just got out of high school. You hadn't started to college," she said.

He waited, and then he raised up onto his arm and turned his head to look at her over his shoulder. "You about finished with that sandwich, Nan?" She was still sitting up in the bed.

She nodded and gave him the saucer.

"I'll turn off the light," he said.

"If you want," she said.

Then he pulled down into the bed again and extended his foot until it touched against hers. He lay still for a minute and then tried to relax.

"Mike, you're not asleep, are you?"

"No," he said. "Nothing like that."

"Well, don't go to sleep before me," she said. "I don't want to be awake by myself."

He didn't answer, but he inched a little closer to her on his side. When she put her arm over him and planted her hand flat against his chest, he took her fingers and squeezed them lightly. But in moments his hand dropped away to the bed, and he sighed.

"Mike? Honey? I wish you'd rub my legs. My legs hurt," she said.

"God," he said softly. "I was sound asleep."

"Well, I wish you'd rub my legs and talk to me. My shoulders hurt, too. But my legs especially."

He turned over and began rubbing her legs, then fell asleep again with his hand on her hip.

"Mike?"

"What is it, Nan? Tell me what it *is*."

"I wish you'd rub me all over," she said, turning onto her back. "My legs and arms both hurt tonight." She raised her knees to make a tower with the covers.

He opened his eyes briefly in the dark and then shut them. "Growing pains, huh?"

"Oh God, yes," she said, wiggling her toes, glad she had drawn him out. "When I was ten or eleven years old I was as big then as I am now. You should've seen me! I grew so fast in those days my legs and arms hurt me all the time. Didn't you?"

"Didn't I what?"

"Didn't you ever feel yourself growing?"

"Not that I remember," he said.

At last he raised up on his elbow, struck a match, and looked at the clock. He turned his pillow over to the cooler side and lay down again.

She said, "You're asleep, Mike. I wish you'd want to talk."

"All right," he said, not moving.

"Just hold me and get me off to sleep. I can't go to sleep," she said.

He turned over and put his arm over her shoulder as she turned onto her side to face the wall.

"Mike?"

He tapped his toes against her foot.

"Why don't you tell me all the things you like and the things you don't like."

"Don't know any right now," he said. "Tell me if you want," he said.

"If you promise to tell *me*. Is that a promise?"

He tapped her foot again.

"Well . . ." she said and turned onto her back, pleased. "I like good foods, steaks and hash brown potatoes, things like that. I like good books and magazines, riding on trains at night, and those times I flew in an airplane." She stopped. "Of course none of this is in order of preference. I'd have to think about it if it was in the order of preference. But I like that, flying in airplanes. There's a moment as you leave the ground you feel whatever happens is all right." She put her leg across his ankle. "I like staying up late at night and then staying in bed the next morning. I wish we could do that all the time, not just once in a while. And I like sex. I like to be touched now and then when I'm not expecting it. I like going to movies and drinking beer with friends afterward. I like to have friends. I like Janice Hendricks very much. I'd like to go dancing at least once a week. I'd like to have nice clothes all the time. I'd like to be able to buy the kids nice clothes every time they need it without having to wait. Laurie needs a new little outfit right now for Easter. And I'd like to get Gary a little suit or something. He's old enough. I'd like you to have a new suit, too. You really need a new suit more than he does. And I'd like us to have a place of our own. I'd like to stop moving around every year, or every other year. Most of all," she said, "I'd like us both just to live a good honest life without having to worry about money and bills and things like that. You're asleep," she said.

"I'm not," he said.

"I can't think of anything else. You go now. Tell me what you'd like."

"I don't know. Lots of things," he mumbled.

"Well, tell me. We're just talking, aren't we?"

"I wish you'd leave me alone, Nan." He turned over to his side of the bed again and let his arm rest off the edge. She turned too and pressed against him.

"Mike?"

"Jesus," he said. Then: "All right. Let me stretch my legs a minute, then I'll wake up."

In a while she said, "Mike? Are you asleep?" She shook his shoulder gently, but there was no response. She lay there for a time huddled against his body, trying to sleep. She lay quietly at first, without moving, crowded against him and taking only very small, very even breaths. But she could not sleep.

She tried not to listen to his breathing, but it began to make her uncomfortable. There was a sound coming from inside his nose when he breathed. She tried to regulate her breathing so that she could breathe in

94

and out at the same rhythm he did. It was no use. The little sound in his nose made everything no use. There was a webby squeak in his chest too. She turned again and nestled her bottom against his, stretched her arm over to the edge and cautiously put her fingertips against the cold wall. The covers had pulled up at the foot of the bed, and she could feel a draft when she moved her legs. She heard two people coming up the stairs to the apartment next door. Someone gave a throaty laugh before opening the door. Then she heard a chair drag on the floor. She turned again. The toilet flushed next door, and then it flushed again. Again she turned, onto her back this time, and tried to relax. She remembered an article she'd once read in a magazine: If all the bones and muscles and joints in the body could join together in perfect relaxation, sleep would almost certainly come. She took a long breath, closed her eyes, and lay perfectly still, arms straight along her sides. She tried to relax. She tried to imagine her legs suspended, bathed in something gauze-like. She turned onto her stomach. She closed her eyes, then she opened them. She thought of the fingers of her hand lying curled on the sheet in front of her lips. She raised a finger and lowered it to the sheet. She touched the wedding band on her ring finger with her thumb. She turned onto her side and then onto her back again. And then she began to feel afraid, and in one unreasoning moment of longing she prayed to go to sleep.

Please, God, let me go to sleep.

She tried to sleep.

"Mike," she whispered.

There was no answer.

She heard one of the children turn over in the bed and bump against the wall in the next room. She listened and listened but there was no other sound. She laid her hand under her left breast and felt the beat of her heart rising into her fingers. She turned onto her stomach and began to cry, her head off the pillow, her mouth against the sheet. She cried. And then she climbed out over the foot of the bed.

She washed her hands and face in the bathroom. She brushed her teeth. She brushed her teeth and watched her face in the mirror. In the living room she turned up the heat. Then she sat down at the kitchen table, drawing her feet up underneath the nightgown. She cried again. She lit a cigarette from the pack on the table. After a time she walked back to the bedroom and got her robe

She looked in on the children. She pulled the covers up over her son's shoulders. She went back to the living room and sat in the big chair. She paged through a magazine and tried to read. She gazed at the photographs and then she tried to read again. Now and then a car went by on the street outside and she looked up. As each car passed she waited, listening. And then she looked down at the magazine again. There was a stack of magazines in the rack by the big chair. She paged through them all.

When it began to be light outside she got up. She walked to the window. The cloudless sky over the hills was beginning to turn white. The trees and the row of two-story apartment houses across the street were beginning to take shape as she watched. The sky grew whiter, the light expanding rapidly up from behind the hills. Except for the times she had been up with one or another of the children (which she did not count because she had never looked outside, only hurried back to bed or to the kitchen), she had seen few sunrises in her life and those when she was little. She knew that none of them had been like this. Not in pictures she had seen nor in any book she had read had she learned a sunrise was so terrible as this.

She waited and then she moved over to the door and turned the lock and stepped out onto the porch. She closed the robe at her throat. The air was wet and cold. By stages things were becoming very visible. She let her eyes see everything until they fastened on the red winking light atop the radio tower atop the opposite hill.

She went through the dim apartment, back into the bedroom. He was knotted up in the center of the bed, the covers bunched over his shoulders, his head half under the pillow. He looked desperate in his heavy sleep, his arms flung out across her side of the bed, his jaws clenched. As she looked, the room grew very light and the pale sheets whitened grossly before her eyes.

She wet her lips with a sticking sound and got down on her knees. She put her hands out on the bed.

"God," she said. "God, will you help us, God?" she said.

Put Yourself in My Shoes

The telephone rang while he was running the vacuum cleaner. He had worked his way through the apartment and was doing the living room, using the nozzle attachment to get at the cat hairs between the cushions. He stopped and listened and then switched off the vacuum. He went to answer the telephone.

"Hello," he said. "Myers here."

"Myers," she said. "How are you? What are you doing?"

"Nothing," he said. "Hello, Paula."

"There's an office party this afternoon," she said. "You're invited. Dick invited you."

"I don't think I can come," Myers said.

"Dick just this minute said get that old man of yours on the phone. Get him down here for a drink. Get him out of his ivory tower and back into the real world for a while. Dick's funny when he's drinking. Myers?"

"I heard you," Myers said.

Myers used to work for Dick. Dick always talked of going to Paris to write a novel, and when Myers had quit to write a novel, Dick had said he would watch for Myers' name on the best-seller list.

"I can't come now," Myers said.

"We found out some horrible news this morning," Paula continued, as if she had not heard him. "You remember Larry Gudinas. He was still here when you came to work. He helped out on science books for a while, and then they put him in the field, and then they canned him? We heard this morning he committed suicide. He shot himself in the mouth. Can you imagine? Myers?"

"I heard you," Myers said. He tried to remember Larry Gudinas and recalled a tall, stooped man with wire-frame glasses, bright ties, and a receding hairline. He could imagine the jolt, the head snapping back. "Jesus," Myers said. "Well, I'm sorry to hear that."

"Come down to the office, honey, all right?" Paula said. "Everybody is just talking and having some drinks and listening to Christmas music. Come down," she said.

Myers could hear it all at the other end of the line. "I don't want to come down," he said. "Paula?" A few snowflakes drifted past the window as he watched. He rubbed his fingers across the glass and then began to write his name on the glass as he waited.

"What? I heard," she said. "All right," Paula said. "Well, then, why don't we meet at Voyles for a drink? Myers?"

"Okay," he said. "Voyles. All right."

"Everybody here will be disappointed you didn't come," she said. "Dick especially. Dick admires you, you know. He does. He's told me so. He admires your nerve. He said if he had your nerve he would have quit years ago. Dick said it takes nerve to do what you did. Myers?"

"I'm right here," Myers said. "I think I can get my car started. If I can't start it, I'll call you back."

"All right," she said. "I'll see you at Voyles. I'll leave here in five minutes if I don't hear from you."

"Say hello to Dick for me," Myers said.

"I will," Paula said. "He's talking about you."

Myers put the vacuum cleaner away. He walked down the two flights and went to his car, which was in the last stall and covered with snow. He got in, worked the pedal a number of times, and tried the starter. It turned over. He kept the pedal down.

As he drove, he looked at the people who hurried along the sidewalks with shopping bags. He glanced at the gray sky, filled with flakes, and at the tall buildings with snow in the crevices and on the window ledges. He tried to see everything, save it for later. He was between stories, and he felt despicable. He found Voyles, a small bar on a corner next to a men's clothing store. He parked in back and went inside. He sat at the bar for a time and then carried a drink over to a little table near the door.

When Paula came in she said, "Merry Christmas," and he got up and gave her a kiss on the cheek. He held a chair for her.

He said, "Scotch?"

"Scotch," she said, then "Scotch over ice" to the girl who came for her order.

Paula picked up his drink and drained the glass.

"I'll have another one, too," Myers said to the girl. "I don't like this place," he said after the girl had moved away.

"What's wrong with this place?" Paula said. "We always come here."

"I just don't like it," he said. "Let's have a drink and then go someplace else."

"Whatever you want," she said.

The girl arrived with the drinks. Myers paid her, and he and Paula touched glasses.

Myers stared at her.

"Dick says hello," she said.

Myers nodded.

Paula sipped her drink. "How was your day today?"

Myers shrugged.

"What'd you do?" she said.

"Nothing," he said. "I vacuumed."

She touched his hand. "Everybody said to tell you hi."

They finished their drinks.

"I have an idea," she said. "Why don't we stop and visit the Morgans for a few minutes. We've never met them, for God's sake, and they've been back for months. We could just drop by and say hello, we're the Myerses. Besides, they sent us a card. They asked us to stop by during the holidays. They *invited* us. I don't want to go home," she finally said and fished in her purse for a cigarette.

Myers recalled setting the furnace and turning out all the lights before he had left. And then he thought of the snow drifting past the window.

"What about that insulting letter they sent telling us they heard we were keeping a cat in the house?" he said.

"They've forgotten about that by now," she said. "That wasn't anything serious, anyway. Oh, let's do it, Myers! Let's go by."

"We should call first if we're going to do anything like that," he said.

"No," she said. "That's part of it. Let's not call. Let's just go knock on the door and say hello, we used to live here. All right? Myers?"

"I think we should call first," he said.

"It's the holidays," she said, getting up from her chair. "Come on, baby."

She took his arm and they went out into the snow. She suggested they take her car and pick up his car later. He opened the door for her and then went around to the passenger's side.

Something took him when he saw the lighted windows, saw snow on the roof, saw the station wagon in the driveway. The curtains were open and Christmas-tree lights blinked at them from the window.

They got out of the car. He held her elbow as they stepped over a pile of snow and started up the walk to the front porch. They had gone a few steps when a large bushy dog hurtled around the corner of the garage and headed straight for Myers.

"Oh, God," he said, hunching, stepping back, bringing his hands up. He slipped on the walk, his coat flapped, and he fell onto the frozen grass with the dread certainty that the dog would go for his throat. The dog growled once and then began to sniff Myers' coat.

Paula picked up a handful of snow and threw it at the dog. The porch light came on, the door opened, and a man called, "Buzzy!" Myers got to his feet and brushed himself off.

"What's going on?" the man in the doorway said. "Who is it? Buzzy, come here, fellow. Come here!"

"We're the Myerses," Paula said. "We came to wish you a Merry Christmas."

"The Myerses?" the man in the doorway said. "Get out! Get in the garage, Buzzy. Get, get! It's the Myerses," the man said to the woman who stood behind him trying to look past his shoulder.

"The Myerses," she said. "Well, ask them in, ask them in, for heaven's sake." She stepped onto the porch and said, "Come in, please, it's freezing. I'm Hilda Morgan and this is Edgar. We're happy to meet you. Please come in."

They all shook hands quickly on the front porch. Myers and Paula stepped inside and Edgar Morgan shut the door.

"Let me have your coats. Take off your coats," Edgar Morgan said. "You're all right?" he said to Myers, observing him closely, and Myers nodded. "I knew that dog was crazy, but he's never pulled anything like this. I saw it. I was looking out the window when it happened."

This remark seemed odd to Myers, and he looked at the man. Edgar Morgan was in his forties, nearly bald, and was dressed in slacks and a sweater and was wearing leather slippers.

"His name is Buzzy," Hilda Morgan announced and made a face. "It's

Edgar's dog. I can't have an animal in the house myself, but Edgar bought this dog and promised to keep him outside."

"He sleeps in the garage," Edgar Morgan said. "He begs to come in the house, but we can't allow it, you know." Morgan chuckled. "But sit down, sit down, if you can find a place with this clutter. Hilda, dear, move some of those things off the couch so Mr and Mrs Myers can sit down."

Hilda Morgan cleared the couch of packages, wrapping paper, scissors, a box of ribbons, bows. She put everything on the floor.

Myers noticed Morgan staring at him again, not smiling now.

Paula said, "Myers, there's something in your hair, dearest."

Myers put a hand up to the back of his head and found a twig and put it in his pocket.

"That dog," Morgan said and chuckled again. "We were just having a hot drink and wrapping some last-minute gifts. Will you join us in a cup of holiday cheer? What would you like?"

"Anything is fine," Paula said.

"Anything," Myers said. "We wouldn't have interrupted."

"Nonsense," Morgan said. "We've been . . . very curious about the Myerses. You'll have a hot drink, sir?"

"That's fine," Myers said.

"Mrs Myers?" Morgan said.

Paula nodded.

"Two hot drinks coming up," Morgan said. "Dear, I think we're ready too, aren't we?" he said to his wife. "This is certainly an occasion."

He took her cup and went out to the kitchen. Myers heard the cupboard door bang and heard a muffled word that sounded like a curse. Myers blinked. He looked at Hilda Morgan, who was settling herself into a chair at the end of the couch.

"Sit down over here, you two," Hilda Morgan said. She patted the arm of the couch. "Over here, by the fire. We'll have Mr Morgan build it up again when he returns." They sat. Hilda Morgan clasped her hands in her lap and leaned forward slightly, examining Myers' face.

The living room was as he remembered it, except that on the wall behind Hilda Morgan's chair he saw three small framed prints. In one print a man in a vest and frock coat was tipping his hat to two ladies who held parasols. All this was happening on a broad concourse with horses and carriages.

"How was Germany?" Paula said. She sat on the edge of the cushion and held her purse on her knees.

"We loved Germany," Edgar Morgan said, coming in from the kitchen with a tray and four large cups. Myers recognized the cups.

"Have you been to Germany, Mrs Myers?" Morgan asked.

"We want to go," Paula said. "Don't we, Myers? Maybe next year, next summer. Or else the year after. As soon as we can afford it. Maybe as soon as Myers sells something. Myers writes."

"I should think a trip to Europe would be very beneficial to a writer," Edgar Morgan said. He put the cups into coasters. "Please help yourselves." He sat down in a chair across from his wife and gazed at Myers. "You said in your letter you were taking off work to write."

"That's true," Myers said and sipped his drink.

"He writes something almost every day," Paula said.

"Is that a fact?" Morgan said. "That's impressive. What did you write today, may I ask?"

"Nothing," Myers said.

"It's the holidays," Paula said.

"You must be proud of him, Mrs Myers," Hilda Morgan said.

"I am," Paula said.

"I'm happy for you," Hilda Morgan said.

"I heard something the other day that might interest you," Edgar Morgan said. He took out some tobacco and began to fill a pipe. Myers lighted a cigarette and looked around for an ashtray, then dropped the match behind the couch.

"It's a horrible story, really. But maybe you could use it, Mr Myers." Morgan struck a flame and drew on the pipe. "Grist for the mill, you know, and all that," Morgan said and laughed and shook the match. "This fellow was about my age or so. He was a colleague for a couple of years. We knew each other a little, and we had good friends in common. Then he moved out, accepted a position at the university down the way. Well, you know how these things go sometimes – the fellow had an affair with one of his students."

Mrs Morgan made a disapproving noise with her tongue. She reached down for a small package that was wrapped in green paper and began to affix a red bow to the paper.

"According to all accounts, it was a torrid affair that lasted for some months," Morgan continued. "Right up until a short time ago, in fact. A week ago, to be exact. On that day – it was in the evening – he announced to his wife – they'd been married for twenty years – he announced to his wife that he wanted a divorce. You can imagine how the fool woman took it, coming out of the blue like that, so to speak. There was quite a row. The whole family got into it. She ordered him out of the house then and there. But just as the fellow was leaving, his son threw a can of tomato soup at him and hit him in the forehead. It caused a concussion that sent the man to the hospital. His condition is quite serious."

Morgan drew on his pipe and gazed at Myers.

"I've never heard such a story," Mrs Morgan said. "Edgar, that's disgusting."

"Horrible," Paula said.

Myers grinned.

"Now *there's* a tale for you, Mr Myers," Morgan said, catching the grin and narrowing his eyes. "Think of the story you'd have if you could get inside that man's head."

"Or her head," Mrs Morgan said. "The wife's. Think of *her* story. To be betrayed in such fashion after twenty years. Think how she must feel."

"But imagine what the poor *boy* must be going through," Paula said. "Imagine, having almost killed his father."

"Yes, that's all true," Morgan said. "But here's something I don't think any of you has thought about. Think about *this* for a moment. Mr Myers, are you listening? Tell me what you think of this. Put yourself in the shoes of that eighteen-year-old coed who fell in love with a married man. Think about *her* for a moment, and then you see the possibilities for your story."

Morgan nodded and leaned back in the chair with a satisfied expression.

"I'm afraid I don't have any sympathy for her," Mrs Morgan said. "I can imagine the sort she is. We all know what she's like, that kind preys on older men. I don't have any sympathy for him, either – the man, the chaser, no, I don't. I'm afraid my sympathies in this case are entirely with the wife and son."

"It would take a Tolstoy to tell it and tell it *right*," Morgan said. "No less than a Tolstoy. Mr Myers, the water is still hot."

"Time to go," Myers said.

He stood up and threw his cigarette into the fire.

"Stay," Mrs Morgan said. "We haven't gotten acquainted yet. You don't know how we have . . . speculated about you. Now that we're together at last, stay a little while. It's such a pleasant surprise."

"We appreciated the card and your note," Paula said.

"The card?" Mrs Morgan said.

Myers sat down.

"We decided not to mail any cards this year," Paula said. "I didn't get around to it when I should have, and it seemed futile to do it at the last minute."

"You'll have another one, Mrs Myers?" Morgan said, standing in front of her now with his hand on her cup. "You'll set an example for your husband."

"It *was* good," Paula said. "It warms you."

"Right," Morgan said. "It warms you. That's right. Dear, did you hear Mrs Myers? It warms you. That's very good. Mr Myers?" Morgan said and waited. "You'll join us?"

"All right," Myers said and let Morgan take the cup.

The dog began to whine and scratch at the door.

"That dog. I don't know what's gotten into that dog," Morgan said. He went to the kitchen and this time Myers distinctly heard Morgan curse as he slammed the kettle onto a burner.

Mrs Morgan began to hum. She picked up a half-wrapped package, cut a piece of tape, and began sealing the paper.

Myers lighted a cigarette. He dropped the match in his coaster. He looked at his watch.

Mrs Morgan raised her head. "I believe I hear singing," she said. She listened. She rose from her chair and went to the front window. "It is singing. Edgar!" she called.

Myers and Paula went to the window.

"I haven't seen carolers in years," Mrs Morgan said.

"What is it?" Morgan said. He had the tray and cups. "What is it? What's wrong?"

"Nothing's wrong, dear. It's carolers. There they are over there, across the street," Mrs Morgan said.

"Mrs Myers," Morgan said, extending the tray. "Mr Myers. Dear."

"Thank you," Paula said.

"*Muchas gracias,*" Myers said.

Morgan put the tray down and came back to the window with his cup. Young people were gathered on the walk in front of the house across the street, boys and girls with an older, taller boy who wore a muffler and a topcoat. Myers could see the faces at the window across the way – the Ardreys – and when the carolers had finished, Jack Ardrey came to the door and gave something to the older boy. The group moved on down the walk, flashlights bobbing, and stopped in front of another house.

"They won't come here," Mrs Morgan said after a time.

"What? Why won't they come here?" Morgan said and turned to his wife. "What a goddamned silly thing to say! Why won't they come here?"

"I just know they won't," Mrs Morgan said.

"And I say they will," Morgan said. "Mrs Myers, are those carolers going to come here or not? What do you think? Will they return to bless this house? We'll leave it up to you."

Paula pressed closer to the window. But the carolers were far down the street now. She did not answer.

"Well, now that all the excitement is over," Morgan said and went over to his chair. He sat down, frowned, and began to fill his pipe.

Myers and Paula went back to the couch. Mrs Morgan moved away from the window at last. She sat down. She smiled and gazed into her cup. Then she put the cup down and began to weep.

Morgan gave his handkerchief to his wife. He looked at Myers. Presently Morgan began to drum on the arm of his chair. Myers moved his feet. Paula looked into her purse for a cigarette. "See what you've caused?" Morgan said as he stared at something on the carpet near Myers' shoes.

Myers gathered himself to stand.

"Edgar, get them another drink," Mrs Morgan said as she dabbed at her eyes. She used the handkerchief on her nose. "I want them to hear about Mrs Attenborough. Mr Myers writes. I think he might appreciate this. We'll wait until you come back before we begin the story."

Morgan collected the cups. He carried them into the kitchen. Myers heard dishes clatter, cupboard doors bang. Mrs Morgan looked at Myers and smiled faintly.

"We have to go," Myers said. "We have to go. Paula, get your coat."

"No, no, we insist, Mr Myers," Mrs Morgan said. "We want you to hear about Mrs Attenborough, poor Mrs Attenborough. You might appreciate this story, too, Mrs Myers. This is your chance to see how your husband's mind goes to work on raw material."

Morgan came back and passed out the hot drinks. He sat down quickly.

"Tell them about Mrs Attenborough, dear," Mrs Morgan said.

"That dog almost tore my leg off," Myers said and was at once surprised at his words. He put his cup down.

"Oh, come, it wasn't that bad," Morgan said. "I saw it."

"You know writers," Mrs Morgan said to Paula. "They like to exaggerate."

"The power of the pen and all that," Morgan said.

"That's it," Mrs Morgan said. "Bend your pen into a plowshare, Mr Myers."

"We'll let Mrs Morgan tell the story of Mrs Attenborough," Morgan said, ignoring Myers, who stood up at that moment. "Mrs Morgan was intimately connected with the affair. I've already told you of the fellow who was knocked for a loop by a can of soup." Morgan chuckled. "We'll let Mrs Morgan tell this one."

"You tell it, dear. And Mr Myers, you listen closely," Mrs Morgan said.

"We have to go," Myers said. "Paula, let's go."

"Talk about honesty," Mrs Morgan said.

"Let's talk about it," Myers said. Then he said, "Paula, are you coming?"

"I want you to hear this story," Morgan said, raising his voice. "You will insult Mrs Morgan, you will insult us both, if you don't listen to this story." Morgan clenched his pipe.

"Myers, please," Paula said anxiously. "I want to hear it. Then we'll go. Myers? Please, honey, sit down for another minute."

Myers looked at her. She moved her fingers, as if signaling him. He hesitated, and then he sat next to her.

Mrs Morgan began. "One afternoon in Munich, Edgar and I went to the Dortmunder Museum. There was a *Bauhaus* exhibit that fall, and Edgar said the heck with it, let's take a day off – he was doing his research, you see – the heck with it, let's take a day off. We caught a tram and rode across Munich to the museum. We spent several hours viewing the exhibit and revisiting some of the galleries to pay homage to a few of our favorites amongst the old masters. Just as we were to leave, I stepped into the ladies' room. I left my purse. In the purse was Edgar's monthly check from home that had come the day before and a hundred and twenty dollars cash that I was going to deposit along with the check. I also had my identification cards in the purse. I did not miss my purse until we arrived home. Edgar immediately telephoned the museum authorities. But while he was talking I saw a taxi out front. A well-dressed woman with white hair got out. She was a stout woman and she was carrying two purses. I called for Edgar and went to the door. The woman introduced herself as Mrs Attenborough, gave me my purse, and explained that she too had visited the museum that afternoon and while in the ladies' room had noticed a purse in the trash can. She of course had opened the purse in an effort to trace the owner. There were the identification cards and such giving our local address. She immediately left the museum and took a taxi in order to deliver the purse herself. Edgar's check was there, but the money, the one hundred twenty dollars, was gone. Nevertheless, I was grateful the other things were intact. It was nearly four o'clock and we asked the woman to stay for tea. She sat down, and after a little while she began to tell us about herself. She had been born and reared in Australia, had married young, had had three children, all sons, been widowed, and still lived in Australia with two of her sons. They raised sheep and had more than twenty thousand acres of land for the sheep to run in, and many drovers and shearers and such who worked for them at certain times of the year. When she came to our home in Munich, she was then on her way to Australia from England, where she had been to visit her youngest son, who was a barrister. She was returning to Australia when we met her," Mrs Morgan said. "She was seeing some of the world in the process. She had many places yet to visit on her itinerary."

"Come to the point, dear," Morgan said.

"Yes. Here is what happened, then. Mr Myers, I'll go right to the climax, as you writers say. Suddenly, after we had had a very pleasant conversation for an hour, after this woman had told about herself and her adventurous life Down Under, she stood up to go. As she started to pass me her cup, her mouth flew open, the cup dropped, and she fell across our couch and died. Died. Right in our living room. It was the most shocking moment in our lives."

Morgan nodded solemnly.

"God," Paula said.

"Fate sent her to die on the couch in our living room in Germany," Mrs Morgan said.

Myers began to laugh. "Fate . . . sent . . . her . . . to . . . die . . . in . . . your . . . living . . . room?" he said between gasps.

"Is that funny, sir?" Morgan said. "Do you find that amusing?"

Myers nodded. He kept laughing. He wiped his eyes on his shirt sleeve. "I'm really sorry," he said. "I can't help it. That line *Fate sent her to die on the couch in our living room in Germany*.' I'm sorry. Then what happened?" he managed to say. "I'd like to know what happened then."

"Mr Myers, we didn't know what to do," Mrs Morgan said. "The shock was terrible. Edgar felt for her pulse, but there was no sign of life. And she had begun to change color. Her face and hands were turning *gray*. Edgar went to the phone to call someone. Then he said, 'Open her purse, see if you can find where she's staying.' All the time averting my eyes from the poor thing there on the couch, I took up her purse. Imagine my complete surprise and bewilderment, my utter bewilderment, when the first thing I saw inside was my hundred twenty dollars, still fastened with the paper clip. I was never so astonished."

"And disappointed," Morgan said. "Don't forget that. It was a keen disappointment."

Myers giggled.

"If you were a real writer, as you say you are, Mr Myers, you would not laugh," Morgan said as he got to his feet. "You would not dare laugh! You would try to understand. You would plumb the depths of that poor soul's heart and try to understand. But you are no writer, sir!"

Myers kept on giggling.

Morgan slammed his fist on the coffee table and the cups rattled in the coasters. "The real story lies right here, in this house, this very living room, and it's time it was told! The real story is *here*, Mr Myers," Morgan said. He walked up and down over the brilliant wrapping paper that had unrolled and now lay spread across the carpet. He stopped to glare at Myers, who was holding his forehead and shaking with laughter.

"Consider *this* for a possibility, Mr Myers!" Morgan screamed. "*Consider!* A friend – let's call him Mr X – is friends with . . . with Mr and Mrs Y, *as well as* Mr and Mrs Z. Mr and Mrs Y and Mr and Mrs Z do not know each other, unfortunately. I say *unfortunately* because if they *had* known each other this story would not exist because it would never have taken place. Now, Mr X learns that Mr and Mrs Y are going to Germany for a year and need someone to occupy their house during the time they are gone. Mr and Mrs Z are looking for suitable accommodations, and Mr X tells them he knows of just the place. But before Mr X can put Mr and Mrs Z in touch with Mr and Mrs Y, the Ys have to leave sooner than expected. Mr X, being a friend, is left to rent the house at his discretion to anyone, including Mr and Mrs Y – I mean Z. Now, Mr and Mrs . . . Z move into the house and bring a cat with them that Mr and Mrs Y hear about later in a letter from Mr X. Mr and Mrs Z bring a cat into the house *even though* the terms of the lease have expressly forbidden cats or other animals in the house because of Mrs Y's asthma. The *real* story, Mr Myers, lies in the situation I've just described. Mr and Mrs Z – I mean Mr and Mrs Y's moving into the Zs' house, *invading* the Zs' house, if the truth is to be told. Sleeping in the Zs' bed is one thing, but unlocking the Zs' private closet and using their linen, vandalizing the things found there, that was against the spirit and letter of the lease. And this *same* couple, the Zs, opened boxes of kitchen utensils marked 'Don't Open'. And broke dishes when it was spelled out, *spelled out* in that same lease, that they were not to use the owners', the Zs' *personal*, I emphasize *personal*, possessions."

Morgan's lips were white. He continued to walk up and down on the paper, stopping every now and then to look at Myers and emit little puffing noises from his lips.

"And the bathroom things, dear – don't forget the bathroom things," Mrs Morgan said. "It's bad enough using the Zs' blankets and sheets, but when they also get into their *bathroom* things and go through the little private things stored in the *attic*, a line has to be drawn."

"That's the *real* story, Mr Myers," Morgan said. He tried to fill his pipe. His hands trembled and tobacco spilled onto the carpet. "That's the real story that is waiting to be written."

"And it doesn't need Tolstoy to tell it," Mrs Morgan said.

"It doesn't need Tolstoy," Morgan said.

Myers laughed. He and Paula got up from the couch at the same time and moved toward the door. "Good night," Myers said merrily.

Morgan was behind him. "If you were a real writer, sir, you would put that story into words and not pussyfoot around with it, either."

Myers just laughed. He touched the doorknob.

"One other thing," Morgan said. "I didn't intend to bring this up, but in light of your behavior here tonight, I want to tell you that I'm missing my two-volume set of 'Jazz at the Philharmonic'. Those records are of great sentimental value. I bought them in 1955. And now I insist you tell me what happened to them!"

"In all fairness, Edgar," Mrs Morgan said as she helped Paula on with her coat, "after you took inventory of the records, you admitted you couldn't recall the last time you had seen those records."

"But I am sure of it now," Morgan said. "I am positive I saw those records just before we left, and now, now I'd like this *writer* to tell me exactly what he knows of their whereabouts. Mr Myers?"

But Myers was already outdoors, and, taking his wife by the hand, he hurried her down the walk to the car. They surprised Buzzy. The dog yelped in what seemed fear and then jumped to the side.

"I insist on *knowing*!" Morgan called. "I am waiting, sir!"

Myers got Paula into the car and started the engine. He looked again at the couple on the porch. Mrs Morgan waved, and then she and Edgar Morgan went back inside and shut the door.

Myers pulled away from the curb.

"Those people are crazy," Paula said.

Myers patted her hand.

"They were scary," she said.

He did not answer. Her voice seemed to come to him from a great distance. He kept driving. Snow rushed at the windshield. He was silent and watched the road. He was at the very end of a story.

Jerry and Molly and Sam

As Al saw it, there was only one solution. He had to get rid of the dog without Betty or the kids finding out about it. At night. It would have to be done at night. He would simply drive Suzy – well, someplace, later he'd decide where – open the door, push her out, drive away. The sooner the better. He felt relieved making the decision. Any action was better than no action at all, he was becoming convinced.

It was Sunday. He got up from the kitchen table where he had been eating a late breakfast by himself and stood by the sink, hands in his pockets. Nothing was going right lately. He had enough to contend with without having to worry about a stinking dog. They were laying off at Aerojet when they should be hiring. The middle of the summer, defense contracts let all over the country and Aerojet was talking of cutting back. *Was* cutting back, in fact, a little more every day. He was no safer than anyone else even though he'd been there two years going on three. He got along with the right people, all right, but seniority or friendship, either one, didn't mean a damn these days. If your number was up, that was that – and there was nothing anybody could do. They got ready to lay off, they laid off. Fifty, a hundred men at a time.

No one was safe, from the foreman and supers right on down to the man on the line. And three months ago, before all the layoffs began, he'd let Betty talk him into moving into this cushy two-hundred-a-month place. Lease, with an option to buy. Shit!

Al hadn't really wanted to leave the other place. He had been comfortable enough. Who could know that two weeks after he'd move they'd start laying off? But who could know anything these days? For example, there was Jill. Jill worked in bookkeeping at Weinstock's. She was a nice girl, said she loved Al. She was just lonely, that's what she told him the first night. She didn't make it a habit, letting herself be picked up by married men, she also told him the first night. He'd met Jill about three months ago, when he was feeling depressed and jittery with all the talk of layoffs just beginning. He met her at the Town and Country, a bar not too far from his new place. They danced a little and he drove her home and they necked in the car in front of her apartment. He had not gone upstairs with her that night, though he was sure he could have. He went upstairs with her the next night.

Now he was having an *affair,* for Christ's sake, and he didn't know what to do about it. He did not want it to go on, and he did not want to break it off: you don't throw everything overboard in a storm. Al was drifting, and he knew he was drifting, and where it was all going to end he could not guess at. But he was beginning to feel he was losing control over everything. Everything. Recently, too, he had caught himself thinking about old age after he'd been constipated a few days – an affliction he had always associated with the elderly. Then there was the matter of the tiny bald spot and of his having just begun to wonder how he would comb his hair a different way. What was he going to do with his life? he wanted to know.

He was thirty-one.

All these things to contend with and then *Sandy,* his wife's younger sister, giving the kids, Alex and Mary, that mongrel dog about four months ago. He wished he'd never seen that dog. Or Sandy, either, for that matter. That bitch! She was always turning up with some shit or other that wound up costing him money, some little flimflam that went haywire after a day or two and *had* to be repaired, something the kids could scream over and fight over and beat the shit out of each other about. God! And then turning right around to touch him, through *Betty,* for twenty-five bucks. The mere thought of all the twenty-five- or fifty-buck checks, and the one just a few months ago for eighty-five to make her car payment – her *car* payment, for God's sake, when he didn't even know if he was going to have a roof over his head – made him want to *kill* the goddamn dog.

Sandy! Betty and Alex and Mary! Jill! And Suzy the goddamn dog! This was Al.

He had to start someplace – setting things in order, sorting all this out. It was time to do something, time for some straight thinking for a change. And he intended to start tonight.

He would coax the dog into the car undetected and, on some pretext or another, go out. Yet he hated to think of the way Betty would lower her eyes as she watched him dress, and then, later, just before he went out the door, ask him where, how long, etc, in a resigned voice that made him feel all the worse. He could never get used to the lying. Besides, he hated to use what little reserve he might have left with Betty by telling her a lie for something different from what she suspected. A wasted lie, so to speak. But he could not tell her the truth, could not say he was *not* going drinking, was *not* going calling on somebody, was instead going to do away with the goddamn dog and thus take the first step toward setting his house in order.

He ran his hand over his face, tried to put it all out of his mind for a minute. He took out a cold half quart of Lucky from the fridge and popped the aluminum top. His life had become a maze, one lie overlaid upon another until he was not sure he could untangle them if he had to.

"The goddamn dog," he said out loud.

"She doesn't have good sense!" was how Al put it. She was a sneak, besides. The moment the back door was left open and everyone gone, she'd pry open the screen, come through to the living room, and urinate on the carpet. There were at least a half dozen map-shaped stains on it right now. But her favorite place was the utility room, where she could root in the dirty clothes, so that all of the shorts and panties now had crotch or seat chewed away. And she chewed through the antenna wires on the outside of the house, and once Al pulled into the drive and found her lying in the front yard with one of his Florsheims in her mouth.

"She's crazy," he'd say. "And she's driving me crazy. I can't make it fast enough to replace it. The sonofabitch, I'm going to kill her one of these days!"

Betty tolerated the dog at greater durations, would go along apparently unruffled for a time, but suddenly she would come upon it, with fists clenched, call it a bastard, a bitch, shriek at the kids about keeping it out of their room, the living room, etc. Betty was that way with the children, too. She could go along with them just so far, let them get away with just so much, and then she would turn on them savagely and slap their faces, screaming, "Stop it! Stop it! I can't stand any more of it!"

But then Betty would say, "It's their first dog. You remember how fond you must have been of your first dog."

"My dog had brains," he would say. "It was an Irish setter!"

* * *

113

The afternoon passed. Betty and the kids returned from someplace or another in the car, and they all had sandwiches and potato chips on the patio. He fell asleep on the grass, and when he woke it was nearly evening.

He showered, shaved, put on slacks and a clean shirt. He felt rested but sluggish. He dressed and he thought of Jill. He thought of Betty and Alex and Mary and Sandy and Suzy. He felt drugged.

"We'll have supper pretty soon," Betty said, coming to the bathroom door and staring at him.

"That's all right. I'm not hungry. Too hot to eat," he said fiddling with his shirt collar. "I might drive over to Carl's, shoot a few games of pool, have a couple of beers."

She said, "I see."

He said, "Jesus!"

She said, "Go ahead, I don't care."

He said, "I won't be gone long."

She said, "Go ahead, I said. I said I don't care."

In the garage, he said, "Goddamn you all!" and kicked the rake across the cement floor. Then he lit a cigarette and tried to get hold of himself. He picked up the rake and put it away where it belonged. He was muttering to himself, saying, "Order, order," when the dog came up to the garage, sniffed around the door, and looked in.

"Here. Come here, Suzy. Here, girl," he called.

The dog wagged her tail but stayed where she was.

He went over to the cupboard above the lawn mower and took down one, then two, and finally three cans of food.

"All you want tonight, Suzy, old girl. All you can eat," he coaxed, opening up both ends of the first can and sliding the mess into the dog's dish.

He drove around for nearly an hour, not able to decide on a place. If he dropped her off in just any neighborhood and the pound were called, the dog would be back in the house in a day or two. The county pound was the first place Betty would call. He remembered reading stories about lost dogs finding their way hundreds of miles back home again. He remembered crime programs where someone saw a license number, and the thought made his heart jump. Held up to public view, without all the facts being in, it'd be a shameful thing to be caught abandoning a dog. He would have to find the right place.

He drove over near the American River. The dog needed to get out more anyway, get the feel of the wind on its back, be able to swim and wade in the river when it wanted; it was a pity to keep a dog fenced in all the time. But the fields near the levee seemed too desolate, no houses around at all. After all, he did want the dog to be found and cared for. A large old two-story house was what he had in mind, with happy, well-behaved reasonable children who needed a dog, who desperately needed a dog. But there were no old two-story houses here, not a one.

He drove back onto the highway. He had not been able to look at the dog since he'd managed to get her into the car. She lay quietly on the back seat now. But when he pulled off the road and stopped the car, she sat up and whined, looking around.

He stopped at a bar, rolled all the car windows down before he went inside. He stayed nearly an hour, drinking beer and playing the shuffle-board. He kept wondering if he should have left all the doors ajar too. When he went back outside, Suzy sat up in the seat and rolled her lips back, showing her teeth.

He got in and started off again.

Then he thought of the place. The neighborhood where they used to live, swarming with kids and just across the line in Yolo County, that would be just the right place. If the dog were picked up, it would be taken to the Woodland Pound, not the pound in Sacramento. Just drive onto one of the streets in the old neighborhood, stop, throw out a handful of the shit she ate, open the door, a little assistance in the way of a push, and out she'd go while he took off. Done! It would be done.

He stepped on it getting out there.

There were porch lights on and at three or four houses he saw men and women sitting on the front steps as he drove by. He cruised along, and when he came to his old house he slowed down almost to a stop and stared at the front door, the porch, the lighted windows. He felt even more insub-stantial, looking at the house. He had lived there – how long? A year, sixteen months? Before that, Chico, Red Bluff, Tacoma, Portland – where he'd met Betty – Yakima . . . Toppenish, where he was born and went to high school. Not since he was a kid, it seemed to him, had he known what it was to be free from worry and worse. He thought of summers fishing and camping in the Cascades, autumns when he'd hunt pheasants behind Sam, the setter's flashing red coat a beacon through cornfields and alfalfa meadows where the boy that he was and the dog that he had would both run like mad. He wished he could keep driving and driving tonight until he was driving onto the old bricked main street of Toppenish, turning left at the first light, then left again, stopping when he came to where his mother lived, and never, never, for any reason ever, ever leave again.

He came to the darkened end of the street. There was a large empty field straight ahead and the street turned to the right, skirting it. For almost a block there were no houses on the side nearer the field and only one house, completely dark, on the other side. He stopped the car and, without thinking any longer about what he was doing, scooped a handful of dog food up, leaned over the seat, opened the back door nearer the field, threw the stuff out, and said, "Go on, Suzy." He pushed her until she jumped down reluctantly. He leaned over farther, pulled the door shut, and drove off, slowly. Then he drove faster and faster.

He stopped at Dupee's, the first bar he came to on the way back to Sacramento. He was jumpy and perspiring. He didn't feel exactly unburdened or relieved, as he had thought he would feel. But he kept assuring himself it was a step in the right direction, that the good feeling would settle on him tomorrow. The thing to do was to wait it out.

After four beers a girl in a turtleneck sweater and sandals and carrying a suitcase sat down beside him. She set the suitcase between the stools. She seemed to know the bartender, and the bartender had something to say to her whenever he came by, once or twice stopping briefly to talk. She told Al her name was Molly, but she wouldn't let him buy her a beer. Instead, she offered to eat half a pizza.

He smiled at her, and she smiled back. He took out his cigarettes and his lighter and put them on the bar.

"Pizza it is!" he said.

Later, he said, "Can I give you a lift somewhere?"

"No, thanks. I'm waiting for someone," she said.

He said, "Where you heading for?"

She said, "No place. Oh," she said, touching the suitcase with her toe, "you mean that?" laughing. "I live here in West Sac. I'm not going anyplace. It's just a washing-machine motor inside belongs to my mother.

Jerry – that's the bartender – he's good at fixing things. Jerry said he'd fix it for nothing."

Al got up. He weaved a little as he leaned over her. He said, "Well, goodbye, honey. I'll see you around."

"You bet!" she said. "And thanks for the pizza. Hadn't eaten since lunch. Been trying to take some of this off." She raised her sweater, gathered a handful of flesh at the waist.

"Sure I can't give you a lift someplace?" he said.

The woman shook her head.

In the car again, driving, he reached for his cigarettes and then, frantically, for his lighter, remembering leaving everything on the bar. The hell with it, he thought, let her have it. Let her put the lighter and the cigarettes in the suitcase along with the washing machine. He chalked it up against the dog, one more expense. But the last, by God! It angered him now, now that he was getting things in order, that the girl hadn't been more friendly. If he'd been in a different frame of mind, he could have picked her up. But when you're depressed, it shows all over you, even the way you light a cigarette.

He decided to go see Jill. He stopped at a liquor store and bought a pint of whiskey and climbed the stairs to her apartment and he stopped at the landing to catch his breath and to clean his teeth with his tongue. He could still taste the mushrooms from the pizza, and his mouth and throat were seared from the whiskey. He realized that what he wanted to do was to go right to Jill's bathroom and use her toothbrush.

He knocked. "It's me, Al," he whispered. "Al," he said louder. He heard her feet hit the floor. She threw the lock and then tried to undo the chain as he leaned heavily against the door.

"Just a minute, honey. Al, you'll have to quit pushing – I can't unhook it. There," she said and opened the door, scanning his face as she took him by the hand.

They embraced clumsily, and he kissed her on the cheek.

"Sit down, honey. Here." She switched on a lamp and helped him to the couch. Then she touched her fingers to her curlers and said, "I'll put on some lipstick. What would you like in the meantime? Coffee? Juice? A beer? I think I have some beer. What do you have there . . . whiskey? What would you like, honey?" She stroked his hair with one hand and leaned over him, gazing into his eyes. "Poor baby, what would you like?" she said.

"Just want you hold me," he said. "Here. Sit down. No lipstick," he said, pulling her onto his lap. "Hold. I'm falling," he said.

She put an arm around his shoulders. She said, "You come on over to the bed, baby, I'll give you what you like."

"Tell you, Jill," he said, "skating on thin ice. Crash through any minute . . . I don't know." He stared at her with a fixed, puffy expression that he could feel but not correct. "Serious," he said.

She nodded. "Don't think about anything, baby. Just relax," she said. She pulled his face to hers and kissed him on the forehead and then the lips. She turned slightly on his lap and said, "No, don't move, Al," the fingers of both hands suddenly slipping around the back of his neck and gripping his face at the same time. His eyes wobbled around the room an instant, then tried to focus on what she was doing. She held his head in place in her strong fingers. With her thumbnails she was squeezing out a blackhead to the side of his nose.

"Sit still!" she said.

"No," he said. "Don't! Stop! Not in the mood for that."

"I almost have it. Sit still, I said! . . . There, look at that. What do you think of that? Didn't know that was there, did you? Now just one more, a big one, baby. The last one," she said.

"Bathroom," he said, forcing her off, freeing his way.

At home it was all tears, confusion. Mary ran out to the car, crying, before he could get parked.

"Suzy's gone," she sobbed. "Suzy's gone. She's never coming back, Daddy, I know it. She's gone!"

My God, heart lurching. *What have I done?*

"Now don't worry, sweetheart. She's probably just off running around somewhere. She'll be back," he said.

"She isn't, Daddy. I know she isn't. Mama said we may have to get another dog."

"Wouldn't that be all right, honey?" he said. "Another dog, if Suzy doesn't come back? We'll go to the pet store —"

"I don't want another dog!" the child cried, holding onto his leg.

"Can we have a monkey, Daddy, instead of a dog?" Alex asked. "If we go to the pet store to look for a dog, can we have a monkey instead?"

"I don't want a monkey!" Mary cried. "I want Suzy."

"Everybody let go now, let Daddy in the house. Daddy has a terrible, terrible headache," he said.

Betty lifted a casserole dish from the oven. She looked tired, irritable ... older. She didn't look at him. "The kids tell you? Suzy's gone? I've combed the neighborhood. Everywhere, I swear."

"That dog'll turn up," he said. "Probably just running around somewhere. That dog'll come back," he said.

"Seriously," she said, turning to him with her hands on her hips, "I think it's something else. I think she might have got hit by a car. I want you to drive around. The kids called her last night, and she was gone then. That's the last's been seen of her. I called the pound and described her to them, but they said all their trucks aren't in yet. I'm supposed to call again in the morning."

He went into the bathroom and could hear her still going on. He began to run the water in the sink, wondering, with a fluttery sensation in his stomach, how grave exactly was his mistake. When he turned off the faucets, he could still hear her. He kept staring at the sink.

"Did you hear me?" she called. "I want you to drive around and look for her after supper. The kids can go with you and look too ... Al?"

"Yes, yes," he answered.

"What?" she said. "What'd you say?"

"I said yes. Yes! All right. Anything! Just let me wash up first, will you?"

She looked through from the kitchen. "Well, what in the hell is eating you? I didn't ask you to get drunk last night, did I? I've had enough of it, I can tell you! I've had a hell of a day, if you want to know. Alex waking me up at five this morning getting in with me, telling me his daddy was snoring so loud that ... that you *scared* him! I saw you out there with your clothes on passed out and the room smelling to high heaven. I tell you, I've had enough of it!" She looked around the kitchen quickly, as if to seize something.

He kicked the door shut. Everything was going to hell. While he was shaving, he stopped once and held the razor in his hand and looked at himself in the mirror: his face doughy, characterless – *immoral,* that was the word. He laid the razor down. *I believe I have made the gravest mistake this time. I believe I have made the gravest mistake of all.* He brought the razor up to his throat and finished.

* * *

He did not shower, did not change clothes. "Put my supper in the oven for me," he said. "Or in the refrigerator. I'm going out. Right now," he said.

"You can wait till after supper. The kids can go with you."

"No, the hell with that. Let the kids eat supper, look around here if they want. I'm not hungry, and it'll be dark soon."

"Is everybody going crazy?" she said. "I don't know what's going to happen to us. I'm ready for a nervous breakdown. I'm ready to lose my mind. What's going to happen to the kids if I lose my mind?" She slumped against the draining board, her face crumpled, tears rolling off her cheeks. "You don't love them, anyway! You never have. It isn't the dog I'm worried about. It's us! It's us! I know you don't love me any more – goddamn you! – but you don't even love the kids!"

"Betty, Betty!" he said. "My God!" he said. "Everything's going to be all right. I promise you," he said. "Don't worry," he said. "I promise you, things'll be all right. I'll find the dog and then things will be all right," he said.

He bounded out of the house, ducked into the bushes as he heard his children coming: the girl crying, saying, "Suzy, Suzy"; the boy saying maybe a train ran over her. When they were inside the house, he made a break for the car.

He fretted at all the lights he had to wait for, bitterly resented the time lost when he stopped for gas. The sun was low and heavy, just over the squat range of hills at the far end of the valley. At best, he had an hour of daylight.

He saw his whole life a ruin from here on in. If he lived another fifty years – hardly likely – he felt he'd never get over it, abandoning the dog. He felt he was finished if he didn't find the dog. A man who would get rid of a little dog wasn't worth a damn. That kind of man would do anything, would stop at nothing.

He squirmed in the seat, kept staring into the swollen face of the sun as it moved lower into the hills. He knew the situation was all out of proportion now, but he couldn't help it. He knew he must somehow retrieve the dog, as the night before he had known he must lose it.

"I'm the one going crazy," he said and then nodded his head in agreement.

* * *

He came in the other way this time, by the field where he had let her off, alert for any sign of movement.

"Let her be there," he said.

He stopped the car and searched the field. Then he drove on, slowly. A station wagon with the motor idling was parked in the drive of the lone house, and he saw a well-dressed woman in heels come out the front door with a little girl. They stared at him as he passed. Farther on he turned left, his eyes taking in the street and the yards on each side as far down as he could see. Nothing. Two kids with bicycles a block away stood beside a parked car.

"Hi," he said to the two boys as he pulled up alongside. "You fellows see anything of a little white dog around today? A kind of white shaggy dog? I lost one."

One boy just gazed at him. The other said, "I saw a lot of little kids playing with a dog over there this afternoon. The street the other side of this one. I don't know what kind of dog it was. It was white maybe. There was a lot of kids."

"Okay, good. Thanks," Al said. "Thank you very very much," he said.

He turned right at the end of the street. He concentrated on the street ahead. The sun had gone down now. It was nearly dark. Houses pitched side by side, trees, lawns, telephone poles, parked cars, it struck him as serene, untroubled. He could hear a man calling his children; he saw a woman in an apron step to the lighted door of her house.

"Is there still a chance for me?" Al said. He felt tears spring to his eyes. He was amazed. He couldn't help but grin at himself and shake his head as he got out his handkerchief. Then he saw a group of children coming down the street. He waved to get their attention.

"You kids see anything of a little white dog?" Al said to them.

"Oh sure," one boy said. "Is it your dog?"

Al nodded.

"We were just playing with him about a minute ago, down the street. In Terry's yard." The boy pointed. "Down the street."

"You got kids?" one of the little girls spoke up.

"I do," Al said.

"Terry said he's going to keep him. He don't have a dog," the boy said.

"I don't know," Al said. "I don't think my kids would like that.

It belongs to them. It's just lost," Al said.

He drove on down the street. It was dark now, hard to see, and he began to panic again, cursing silently. He swore at what a weathervane he was, changing this way and that, one moment this, the next moment that.

He saw the dog then. He understood he had been looking at it for a time. The dog moved slowly, nosing the grass along a fence. Al got out of the car, started across the lawn, crouching forward as he walked, calling, "Suzy, Suzy, Suzy."

The dog stopped when she saw him. She raised her head. He sat down on his heels, reached out his arm, waiting. They looked at each other. She moved her tail in greeting. She lay down with her head between her front legs and regarded him. He waited. She got up. She went around the fence and out of sight.

He sat there. He thought he didn't feel so bad, all things considered. The world was full of dogs. There were dogs and there were dogs. Some dogs you just couldn't do anything with.

Why, Honey?

Dear Sir,

I was so surprised to receive your letter asking about my son, how did you know I was here? I moved here years ago right after it started to happen. No one knows who I am here but I'm afraid all the same. Who I am afraid of is him. When I look at the paper I shake my head and wonder. I read what they write about him and I ask myself is that man really my son, is he really doing these things?

He was a good boy except for his outbursts and that he could not tell the truth. I can't give you any reasons. It started one summer over the Fourth of July, he would have been about fifteen. Our cat Trudy disappeared and was gone all night and the next day. Mrs Cooper who lives behind us came the next evening to tell me Trudy crawled into her backyard that afternoon to die. Trudy was cut up she said but she recognized Trudy. Mr Cooper buried the remains.

Cut up? I said. What do you mean cut up?

Mr Cooper saw two boys in the field putting firecrackers in Trudy's ears and in her you know what. He tried to stop them but they ran.

Who, who would do such a thing, did he see who it was?

He didn't know the other boy but one of them ran this way. Mr Cooper thought it was your son.

I shook my head. No, that's just not so, he wouldn't do a thing like that, he loved Trudy, Trudy has been in the family for years, no, it wasn't my son.

That evening I told him about Trudy and he acted surprised and shocked and said we should offer a reward. He typed something up and promised to post it at school. But just as he was going to his room that night he said don't take it too hard, mom, she was old, in cat years she was sixty-five or seventy, she lived a long time.

He went to work afternoons and Saturdays as a stockboy at Hartley's. A friend of mine who worked there, Betty Wilks, told me about the job and said she would put in a word for him. I mentioned it to him that evening and he said good, jobs for young people are hard to find.

The night he was to draw his first check I cooked his favorite supper and had everything on the table when he walked in. Here's the man of the house, I said, hugging him. I am so proud, how much did you draw, honey? Eighty dollars, he said. I was flabbergasted. That's wonderful, honey, I just cannot believe it. I'm starved, he said, let's eat.

I was happy, but I couldn't understand it, it was more than I was making.

When I did the laundry I found the stub from Hartley's in his pocket, it was for twenty-eight dollars, he said eighty. Why didn't he just tell the truth? I couldn't understand.

I would ask him where did you go last night, honey? To the show he would answer. Then I would find out he went to the school dance or spent the evening riding around with somebody in a car. I would think what difference could it make, why doesn't he just be truthful, there is no reason to lie to his mother.

I remember once he was supposed to have gone on a field trip, so I asked him what did you see on the field trip, honey? And he shrugged and said land formations, volcanic rock, ash, they showed us where there used to be a big lake a million years ago, now it's just a desert. He looked me in the eyes and went on talking. Then I got a note from the school the next day saying they wanted permission for a field trip, could he have permission to go.

Near the end of his senior year he bought a car and was always gone. I was concerned about his grades but he only laughed. You know he was an excellent student, you know that about him if you know anything. After that he bought a shotgun and a hunting knife.

I hated to see those things in the house and I told him so. He laughed, he always had a laugh for you. He said he would keep the gun and the knife in the trunk of his car, he said they would be easier to get to there anyway.

One Saturday night he did not come home. I worried myself into a terrible state. About ten o'clock the next morning he came in and asked me to cook him breakfast, he said he had worked up an appetite out hunting, he said he was sorry for being gone all night, he said they had driven a long way to get to this place. It sounded strange. He was nervous.

Where did you go?

Up to the Wenas. We got a few shots.

Who did you go with, honey?

Fred.

Fred?

He stared and I didn't say anything else.

On the Sunday right after I tiptoed into his room for his car keys. He had promised to pick up some breakfast items on his way home from work the night before and I thought he might have left the things in his car. I saw his new shoes sitting half under his bed and covered with mud and sand. He opened his eyes.

Honey, what happened to your shoes? Look at your shoes.

I ran out of gas, I had to walk for gas. He sat up. What do you care?

I am your mother.

While he was in the shower I took the keys and went out to his car. I opened the trunk. I didn't find the groceries. I saw the shotgun lying on a quilt and the knife too and I saw a shirt of his rolled in a ball and I shook it out and it was full of blood. It was wet. I dropped it. I closed the trunk and started back for the house and I saw him watching at the window and he opened the door.

I forgot to tell you, he said, I had a bad bloody nose, I don't know if that shirt can be washed, throw it away. He smiled.

A few days later I asked how he was getting along at work. Fine, he said, he had gotten a raise. But I met Betty Wilks on the street and she said they were all sorry at Hartley's that he had quit, he was so well liked, she said, Betty Wilks.

Two nights after that I was in bed but I couldn't sleep, I stared at the ceiling. I heard his car pull up out front and I listened as he put the key in the lock and he came through the kitchen and down the hall to his room and he shut the door after him. I got up. I could see light under his door, I knocked and pushed on the door and said would you like a hot cup of tea, honey, I can't sleep. He was bent over by the dresser and slammed a drawer and turned on me, get out he screamed, get out of here, I'm sick of you spying he screamed. I went to my room and cried myself to sleep. He broke my heart that night.

The next morning he was up and out before I could see him, but that was all right with me. From then on I was going to treat him like a lodger unless he wanted to mend his ways, I was at my limit. He would have to apologize if he wanted us to be more than just strangers living together under the same roof.

When I came in that evening he had supper ready. How are you? he said, he took my coat. How was your day?

I said I didn't sleep last night, honey. I promised myself I wouldn't bring it up and I'm not trying to make you feel guilty but I'm not used to being talked to like that by my son.

I want to show you something, he said, and he showed me this essay he was writing for his civics class. I believe it was on relations between the congress and the supreme court. (It was the paper that won a prize for him at graduation!) I tried to read it and then I decided, this was the time. Honey, I'd like to have a talk with you, it's hard to raise a child with things the way they are these days, it's especially hard for us having no father in the house, no man to turn to when we need him. You are nearly grown now but I am still responsible and I feel I am entitled to some respect and consideration and have tried to be fair and honest with you. I want the truth, honey, that's all I've ever asked from you, the truth. Honey, I took a breath, suppose you had a child who when you asked him something, anything, where he's been or where he's going, what he's doing with his time, anything, never, he never once told you the truth? Who if you asked him is it raining outside, would answer no, it is nice and sunny, and I guess laugh to himself and think you were too old or too stupid to see his clothes are wet. Why should he lie, you ask yourself, what does he gain I don't understand. I keep asking myself why but I don't have the answer. Why, honey?

He didn't say anything, he kept staring, then he moved over alongside me and said I'll show you. Kneel is what I say, kneel down is what I say, he said, that's the first reason why.

I ran to my room and locked the door. He left that night, he took his things, what he wanted, and he left. Believe it or not I never saw him again. I saw him at his graduation but that was with a lot of people around. I sat in the audience and watched him get his diploma and a prize for his essay, then I heard him give the speech and then I clapped right along with the rest.

I went home after that.

I have never seen him again. Oh sure I have seen him on the TV and I have seen his pictures in the paper.

I found out he joined the marines and then I heard from someone he was out of the marines and going to college back east and then he married that girl and got himself in politics. I began to see his name in the paper. I found out his address and wrote to him, I wrote a letter every few months, there never was an answer. He ran for governor and was elected, and was famous now. That's when I began to worry.

I built up all these fears, I became afraid, I stopped writing him of course and then I hoped he would think I was dead. I moved here. I had them give me an unlisted number. And then I had to change my name. If you are a powerful man and want to find somebody, you can find them, it wouldn't be that hard.

I should be so proud but I am afraid. Last week I saw a car on the street with a man inside I know was watching me, I came straight back and locked the door. A few days ago the phone rang and rang, I was lying down. I picked up the receiver but there was nothing there.

I am old. I am his mother. I should be the proudest mother in all the land but I am only afraid.

Thank you for writing. I wanted someone to know. I am very ashamed.

I also wanted to ask how you got my name and knew where to write, I have been praying no one knew. But you did. Why did you? Please tell me why.

Yours truly,

The Ducks

A wind came up that afternoon, bringing gusts of rain and sending the ducks up off the lake in black explosions looking for the quiet potholes out in the timber. He was at the back of the house splitting firewood and saw the ducks cutting over the highway and dropping into the marsh behind the trees. He watched, groups of half a dozen, but mostly doubles, one bunch behind the other. Out over the lake it was already dark and misty and he could not see the other side, where the mill was. He worked faster, driving the iron wedge down harder into the big dry chunks, splitting them so far down that the rotten ones flew apart. On his wife's clothesline, strung up between the two sugar pines, sheets and blankets popped shotlike in the wind. He made two trips and carried all the wood onto the porch before it started to rain.

"Supper's ready!" she called from the kitchen.

He went inside and washed up. They talked a little while they ate, mostly about the trip to Reno. Three more days of work, then payday, then the weekend in Reno. After supper he went out onto the porch and began sacking up his decoys. He stopped when she came out. She stood there in the doorway watching him.

"You going hunting again in the morning?"

He looked away from her and out toward the lake. "Look at the weather. I think it's going to be good in the morning." Her sheets were snapping in the wind and there was a blanket down on the ground. He nodded at it. "Your things are going to get wet."

"They weren't dry, anyway. They've been out there two days and they're not dry yet."

"What's the matter? Don't you feel good?" he said.

"I feel all right." She went back into the kitchen and shut the door and looked at him through the window. "I just hate to have you gone all the time. It seems like you're gone all the time," she said to the window. Her breath produced itself on the glass, then went away. When he came inside, he put the decoys in the corner and went to get his lunch pail. She was leaning against the cupboard, her hands on the edge of the draining board. He touched her hip, pinched her dress.

"You wait'll we get to Reno. We're going to have some fun," he said.

She nodded. It was hot in the kitchen and there were little drops of sweat over her eyes. "I'll get up when you come in and fix you some breakfast."

"You sleep. I'd rather have you sleep." He reached around behind her for his lunch pail.

"Kiss me bye," she said.

He hugged her. She fastened her arms around his neck and held him. "I love you. Be careful driving."

She went to the kitchen window and watched him running, jumping over the puddles until he got to the pickup. She waved when he looked back from inside the cab. It was almost dark and it was raining hard.

She was sitting in a chair by the living-room window listening to the radio and the rain when she saw the pickup lights turn into the drive. She got up quickly and hurried to the back door. He stood there in the doorway, and she touched his wet, rubbery coat with her fingers.

"They told everybody to go home. The mill boss had a heart attack. He fell right down on the floor up in the mill and died."

"You scared me." She took his lunch pail and shut the door. "Who was it? Was it that foreman named Mel?"

"No, his name was Jack Granger. He was about fifty years old, I guess." He walked over close to the oil stove and stood there warming his hands. "Jesus, it's so funny! He'd come through where I work and asked me how I was doing and probably wasn't gone five minutes when Bill Bessie come through and told me Jack Granger had just died right up in the mill." He shook his head. "Just like that."

"Don't think about it," she said and took his hands between hers and rubbed his fingers.

"I'm not. Just one of them things, I guess. You never know."

The rain rushed against the house and slashed across the windows.

"God, it's hot in here! There any beer?" he said.

"I think there's some left," she said and followed him out to the kitchen.

His hair was still wet and she ran her fingers through it when he sat down. She opened a beer for him and poured some into a cup for herself. He sat drinking it in little sips, looking out the window toward the dark woods.

He said, "One of the guys said he had a wife and two grown kids."

She said, "That Granger man, that's a shame. It's nice to have you home, but I hate for something like that to happen."

"That's what I told some of the boys. I said it's nice to get on to home, but Christ, I hate to have it like this." He edged a little in the chair. "You know, I think most of the men would've gone ahead and worked, but some of the boys up in the mill said they wouldn't work, him laying there like that." He finished off the beer and got up. "I'll tell you – I'm glad they didn't work," he said.

She said, "I'm glad you didn't, either. I had a really funny feeling when you left tonight. I was thinking about it, the funny feeling I had, when I saw the lights."

"He was just in the lunch room last night telling jokes. Granger was a good boy. Always laughing."

She nodded. "I'll fix us something to eat if you'll eat something."

"I'm not hungry, but I'll eat something," he said.

They sat in the living room and held hands and watched television.

"I've never seen any of these programs before," he said.

She said, "I don't much care about watching any more. You can hardly get anything worth watching. Saturday and Sunday it's all right. But there's nothing weeknights."

He stretched his legs and leaned back. He said, "I'm kind of tired. I think I'll go to bed."

She said, "I think I'll take a bath and go to bed, too," She moved her fingers through his hair and dropped her hand and smoothed his neck. "Maybe we'll have a little tonight. We never hardly get a chance to have a little." She touched her other hand to his thigh, leaned over and kissed him. "What do you think about that?"

"That sounds all right," he said. He got up and walked over to the window. Against the trees outside he could see her reflection standing behind him and a little to the side. "Hon, why don't you go ahead and take your bath and we'll turn in," he said. He stood there for a while longer watching the rain beat against the window. He looked at his watch. If he were working, it would be the lunch hour now. He went into the bedroom and began getting undressed.

In his shorts, he walked back into the living room and picked up a book off the floor — *Best-Loved Poems of the American People*. He guessed it had come in the mail from the club she belonged to. He went through the house and turned off the lights. Then he went back into the bedroom. He got under the covers, put her pillow on top of his, and twisted the gooseneck lamp around so that the light fell on the pages. He opened the book to the middle and began to look at some of the poems. Then he laid the book on the bedstand and bent the lamp away toward the wall. He lit a cigarette. He put his arms behind his head and lay there smoking. He looked straight ahead at the wall. The lamplight picked up all of the tiny cracks and swells in the plaster. In a corner, up near the ceiling, there was a cobweb. He could hear the rain washing down off the roof.

She stood up in the tub and began drying herself. When she noticed him watching, she smiled and draped the towel over her shoulder and made a little step in the tub and posed.

"How does it look?"

"All right," he said.

"Okay," she said.

"I thought you were still . . . you know," he said.

"I am." She finished drying and dropped the towel on the floor beside the tub and stepped daintily onto it. The mirror beside her was steamy and the odor of her body carried to him. She turned around and reached up to a shelf for the box. Then she slipped into her belt and adjusted the white pad. She tried to look at him, she tried to smile. He crushed out the cigarette and picked up the book again.

"What are you reading?" she called.

"I don't know. Crap," he said. He turned to the back of the book and began looking through the biographies.

She turned off the light and came out of the bathroom brushing her hair. "You still going in the morning?" she said.

"Guess not," he said.

She said, "I'm glad. We'll sleep in late, then get up and have a big breakfast."

He reached over and got another cigarette.

She put the brush in a drawer, opened another drawer and took out a nightgown.

"Do you remember when you got me this?" she said.

He looked at her in reply.

She came around to his side of the bed. They lay quietly for a time, smoking his cigarette until he nodded he was finished, and then she put it out. He reached over her, kissed her on the shoulder, and switched off the light. "You know," he said, lying back down, "I think I want to get out of here. Go someplace else." She moved over to him and put her leg between his. They lay on their sides facing each other, lips almost touching. He wondered if his breath smelled as clean as hers. He said, "I just want to leave. We been here a long time. I'd like to go back home and see my folks. Or maybe go on up to Oregon. That's good country."

"If that's what you want," she said.

"I think so," he said. "There's a lot of places to go."

She moved a little and took his hand and put it on her breast. Then she opened her mouth and kissed him, pulling his head down with her other hand. Slowly she inched up in the bed, gently moving his head down to her breast. He took the nipple and began working it in his mouth. He tried to think how much he loved her or if he loved her. He could hear her breathing but he could also hear the rain. They lay like this.

She said, "If you don't want to, it's all right."

"It's not that," he said, not knowing what he meant.

He let her go when he could tell she was asleep and turned over to his own side. He tried to think of Reno. He tried to think of the slots and the way the dice clicked and how they looked turning over under the lights. He tried to hear the sound the roulette ball made as it skimmed around the gleaming wheel. He tried to concentrate on the wheel. He looked and looked and listened and listened and heard the saws and the machinery slowing down, coming to a stop.

He got out of bed and went to the window. It was black outside and he could see nothing, not even the rain. But he could hear it, cascading off the roof and into a puddle under the window. He could hear it all over the house. He ran his finger across the drool on the glass.

When he got back into bed, he moved close to her and put his hand on her hip. "Hon, wake up," he whispered. But she only shuddered and moved over farther to her own side. She kept on sleeping. "Wake up," he whispered. "I hear something outside."

How About This?

All the optimism that had colored his flight from the city was gone now, had vanished the evening of the first day, as they drove north through the dark stands of redwood. Now, the rolling pasture land, the cows, the isolated farmhouses of western Washington seemed to hold out nothing for him, nothing he really wanted. He had expected something different. He drove on and on with a rising sense of hopelessness and outrage.

He kept the car at fifty, all that the road allowed. Sweat stood on his forehead and over his upper lip, and there was a sharp heady odor of clover in the air all around them. The land began to change; the highway dipped suddenly, crossed a culvert, rose again, and then the asphalt ran out and he was holding the car on a country dirt road, an astonishing trail of dust rising behind them. As they passed the ancient burned-out foundation of a house set back among some maple trees, Emily removed her dark glasses and leaned forward, staring.

"That *is* the old Owens place," she said. "He and Dad were friends. He kept a still in his attic and had a big team of dray horses he used to enter in all the fairs. He died with a ruptured appendix when I was about ten years old. The house burned down a year later at Christmas. They moved to Bremerton after that."

"Is that so?" he said. "Christmas." Then: "Do I turn right or left here? Emily? Right or left?"

"Left," she said. "Left."

She put on her glasses again, only to take them off a moment later. "Stay on this road, Harry, until you come to another crossroad. Then right. Only a little farther then." She smoked steadily, one cigarette after the other, was silent now as she looked out at the cleared fields, at the isolated stands of fir trees, at the occasional weathered house.

He shifted down, turned right. The road began to drop gradually into a lightly wooded valley. Far ahead – Canada, he supposed – he could see a range of mountains and behind those mountains a darker, still higher range.

"There's a little road," she said, "at the bottom. That's the road."

He turned carefully and drove down the rutted track road slowly, waiting for the first sign of the house. Emily sat next to him, edgy, he could see, smoking again, also waiting for the first glimpse. He blinked his eyes as low shaggy branches slapped the windshield. She leaned forward slightly and touched her hand to his leg. "Now," she said. He slowed almost to a stop, drove through a tiny clear puddle of a stream that came out of the high grass on his left, then into a mass of dogwood that fingered and scraped the length of the car as the little road climbed. "There it is," she said, moving her hand from his leg.

After the first unsettling glance, he kept his eyes on the road. He looked at the house again after he had brought the car to a stop near the front door. Then he licked his lips, turned to her, and tried to smile.

"Well, we're here," he said.

She was looking at him, not looking at the house at all.

Harry had always lived in cities – San Francisco for the last three years, and, before that, Los Angeles, Chicago, and New York. But for a long time he had wanted to move to the country, somewhere in the country. At first he wasn't too clear about where he wanted to go; he just knew he wanted to leave the city to try to start over again. A simpler life was what he had in mind, just the essentials, he said. He was thirty-two years old and was a writer in a way, but he was also an actor and a musician. He played the saxophone, performed occasionally with the Bay City Players, and was writing a first novel. He had been writing the novel since the time he lived in New York. One bleak Sunday afternoon in March, when he had again started talking about a change, a more honest life somewhere in the country, she'd mentioned, jokingly at first, her father's deserted place in the northwestern part of Washington.

"My God," Harry had said, "you wouldn't mind? Roughing it, I mean? Living in the country like that?"

"I was born there," she said, laughing. "Remember? I've lived in the country. It's all right. It has advantages. I could live there again. I don't know about you, though, Harry. If it'd be good for you."

She kept looking at him, serious now. He felt lately that she was always looking at him.

"You wouldn't regret it?" he said. "Giving up things here?"

"I wouldn't be giving up much, would I, Harry?" She shrugged. "But I'm not going to encourage the idea, Harry."

"Could you paint up there?" he asked.

"I can paint anywhere," she said. "And there's Bellingham," she said. "There's a college there. Or else Vancouver or Seattle." She kept watching him. She sat on a stool in front of a shadowy half-finished portrait of a man and woman and rolled two paintbrushes back and forth in her hand.

That was three months ago. They had talked about it and talked about it and now they were here.

He rapped on the walls near the front door. "Solid. A solid foundation. If you have a solid foundation, that's the main thing." He avoided looking at her. She was shrewd and might have read something from his eyes.

"I told you not to expect too much," she said.

"Yes, you did. I distinctly remember," he said, still not looking at her. He gave the bare board another rap with his knuckles and moved over beside her. His sleeves were rolled in the damp afternoon heat, and he was wearing white jeans and sandals. "Quiet, isn't it?"

"A lot different from the city."

"God, yes . . . Pretty up here, too." He tried to smile. "Needs a little work, that's all. A little work. It'll be a good place if we want to stay. Neighbors won't bother us, anyway."

"We had neighbors here when I was a little girl," she said. "You had to drive to see them, but they were neighbors."

The door opened at an angle. The top hinge was loose: nothing much, Harry judged. They moved slowly from room to room. He tried to cover his disappointment. Twice he knocked on the walls and said, "Solid". Or, "They don't make houses like this any more. You can do a lot with a house like this."

She stopped in front of a large room and drew a long breath.

"Yours?"

She shook her head.

"And we could get the necessary furniture we need from your Aunt Elsie?"

"Yes, whatever we need," she said. "That is, if it's what we want, to stay here. I'm not pushing. It's not too late to go back. There's nothing lost."

In the kitchen they found a wood stove and a mattress pushed against one wall. In the living room again, he looked around and said, "I thought it'd have a fireplace."

"I never said it had a fireplace."

"I just had the impression for some reason it would have one. . . No outlets, either," he said a moment later. Then: "No electricity!"

"Toilet, either," she said.

He wet his lips. "Well," he said, turning away to examine something in the corner, "I guess we could fix up one of these rooms with a tub and all, and get someone to do the plumbing work. But electricity is something else, isn't it? I mean, let's face all these things when we come to them. One thing at a time, right? Don't you think? Let's . . . let's not let any of it get us down, okay?"

"I wish you'd just be quiet," she said.

She turned and went outside.

He jumped down the steps a minute later and drew a breath of air and they both lighted cigarettes. A flock of crows got up at the far end of the meadow and flew slowly and silently into the woods. They walked toward the barn, stopping to inspect the withered apple trees. He broke off one of the small dry branches, turned it over and over in his hands while she stood beside him and smoked a cigarette. It was peaceful, more or less appealing country, and he thought it pleasant to feel that something permanent, really permanent, might belong to him. He was taken by a sudden affection for the little orchard.

"Get these bearing again," he said. "Just need water and some looking after's all." He could see himself coming out of the house with a wicker basket and pulling down large red apples, still wet with the morning's dew, and he understood that the idea was attractive to him.

He felt a little cheered as they approached the barn. He examined briefly the old license plates nailed to the door. Green, yellow, white plates from the state of Washington, rusted now, 1922–23–24–25–26–27–28–29–34–36–37–40–41–1949; he studied the dates as if he thought their sequence might disclose a code. He threw the wooden latch and pulled and pushed at the heavy door until it swung open. The air inside smelled unused. But he believed it was not an unpleasant smell.

"It rains a lot here in the winter," she said. "I don't remember it ever being this hot in June." Sunlight stuck down through the splits in the roof. "Once Dad shot a deer out of season. I was about – I don't know – eight or nine, around in there." She turned to him as he stood stopped near the door to look at an old harness that hung from a nail. "Dad was down here in the barn with the deer when the game warden drove into the yard. It was dark. Mother sent me down here for Dad, and the game warden, a big heavyset man with a hat, followed me. Dad was carrying a lamp, just coming down from the loft. He and the game warden talked a few minutes. The deer was hanging there, but the game warden didn't say anything. He offered Dad a chew of tobacco, but Dad refused – he never had liked it and wouldn't take any even then. Then the game warden pulled my ear and left. But I don't want to think about any of that," she added quickly. "I haven't thought about things like that in years. I don't want to make comparisons," she said. "No," she said. She stepped back, shaking her head. "I'm not going to cry. I know that sounds melodramatic and just plain stupid, and I'm sorry for sounding melodramatic and stupid. But the truth is, Harry . . ." She shook her head again. "I don't know. Maybe coming back here was a mistake. I can feel your disappointment."

"You don't know," he said.

"No, that's right, I don't know," she said. "And I'm sorry, I'm really not meaning to try to influence you one way or the other. But I don't think you want to stay. Do you?"

He shrugged.

He took out a cigarette. She took it from him and held it, waiting for a match, waiting for his eyes to meet hers over the match.

"When I was little," she went on, "I wanted to be in a circus when I grew up. I didn't want to be a nurse or a teacher. Or a painter. I didn't want to be a painter then. I wanted to be Emily Horner, High-Wire Artist. It was a big thing with me. I used to practice down here in the barn, walking the rafters. That big rafter up there, I walked that hundreds of times." She started to say something else, but puffed her cigarette and put it out under her heel, tamping it down carefully into the dirt.

Outside the barn he could hear a bird calling, and then he heard a scurrying sound over the boards up in the loft. She walked past him, out into the light, and started slowly through the deep grass toward the house.

"What are we going to do, Emily?" he called after her.

She stopped, and he came up beside her.

"Stay alive," she said. Then she shook her head and smiled faintly. She touched his arm. "Jesus, I guess we are in kind of a spot, aren't we? But that's all I can say, Harry."

"We've got to decide," he said, not really knowing what he meant.

"You decide, Harry, if you haven't already. It's your decision. I'd just as soon go back if that makes it any easier for you. We'll stay with Aunt Elsie a day or two and then go back. All right? But give me a cigarette, will you? I'm going up to the house."

He moved closer to her then and thought they might embrace. He wanted to. But she did not move; she only looked at him steadily, and so he touched her on the nose with his forefinger and said, "I'll see you in a little while."

He watched her go. He looked at his watch, turned, and walked slowly down the pasture toward the woods. The grass came up to his knees. Just before he entered the woods, as the grass began to thin out, he found a sort of path. He rubbed the bridge of his nose under his dark glasses, looked back at the house and the barn, and continued on, slowly. A cloud of mosquitoes moved with his head as he walked. He stopped to light a cigarette. He brushed at the mosquitoes. He looked back again, but now he could not see the house or barn. He stood there smoking, beginning to feel the silence that lay in the grass and in the trees and in the shadows farther back in the trees. Wasn't this what he'd longed for? He walked on, looking for a place to sit.

He lighted another cigarette and leaned against a tree. He picked up some wood chips from the soft dirt between his legs. He smoked. He remembered a volume of plays by Ghelderode lying on top of the things in the back seat of the car, and then he recalled some of the little towns they had driven through that morning – Ferndale, Lynden, Custer. Nooksack. He suddenly recalled the mattress in the kitchen. He understood that it made him afraid. He tried to imagine Emily walking the big rafter in the barn. But that made him afraid too. He smoked. He felt very calm really, all things considered. He wasn't going to stay here, he knew that, but it didn't upset him to know that now. He was pleased he knew himself so well. He would be all right, he decided. He was only thirty-two. Not so old. He was, for the moment, in a spot. He could admit that.

After all, he considered, that was life, wasn't it? He put out the cigarette. In a little while he lit another one.

As he rounded a corner of the house, he saw her completing a cartwheel. She landed with a light thump, slightly crouched, and then she saw him.

"Hey!" she yelled, grinning gravely.

She raised herself onto the balls of her feet, arms out to the sides over her head, and then pitched forward. She turned two more cartwheels while he watched, and then she called, "How about *this*!" She dropped lightly onto her hands and, getting her balance, began a shaky hesitant movement in his direction. Face flushed, blouse hanging over her chin, legs waving insanely, she advanced on him. "Have you decided?" she said, quite breathless.

He nodded.

"So?" she said. She let herself fall against her shoulder and rolled onto her back, covering her eyes from the sun with an arm as if to uncover her breasts.

She said, "Harry."

He was reaching to light a cigarette with his last match when his hands began to tremble. The match went out, and he stood there holding the empty matchbook and the cigarette, staring at the vast expanse of trees at the end of the bright meadow.

"Harry, we have to love each other," she said. "We'll just have to love each other," she said.

Bicycles, Muscles, Cigarettes

It had been two days since Evan Hamilton had stopped smoking, and it seemed to him everything he'd said and thought for the two days somehow suggested cigarettes. He looked at his hands under the kitchen light. He sniffed his knuckles and his fingers.

"I can smell it," he said.

"I know. It's as if it sweats out of you," Ann Hamilton said. "For three days after I stopped I could smell it on me. Even when I got out of the bath. It was disgusting." She was putting plates on the table for dinner. "I'm so sorry, dear. I know what you're going through. But, if it's any consolation, the second day is always the hardest. The third day is hard, too, of course, but from then on, if you can stay with it that long, you're over the hump. But I'm so happy you're serious about quitting, I can't tell you." She touched his arm. "Now, if you'll just call Roger, we'll eat."

Hamilton opened the front door. It was already dark. It was early in November and the days were short and cool. An older boy he had never seen before was sitting on a small, well-equipped bicycle in the driveway. The boy leaned forward just off the seat, the toes of his shoes touching the pavement and keeping him upright.

"You Mr Hamilton?" the boy said.

"Yes, I am," Hamilton said. "What is it? Is it Roger?"

"I guess Roger is down at my house talking to my mother. Kip is there and this boy named Gary Berman. It is about my brother's bike. I don't know for sure," the boy said, twisting the handle grips, "but my mother asked me to come and get you. One of Roger's parents."

"But he's all right?" Hamilton said. "Yes, of course, I'll be right with you."

He went into the house to put his shoes on.

"Did you find him?" Ann Hamilton said.

"He's in some kind of jam," Hamilton answered. "Over a bicycle. Some boy – I didn't catch his name – is outside. He wants one of us to go back with him to his house."

"Is he all right?" Ann Hamilton said and took her apron off.

"Sure, he's all right." Hamilton looked at her and shook his head. "It sounds like it's just a childish argument, and the boy's mother is getting herself involved."

"Do you want me to go?" Ann Hamilton asked.

He thought for a minute. "Yes, I'd rather you went, but I'll go. Just hold dinner until we're back. We shouldn't be long."

"I don't like his being out after dark," Ann Hamilton said. "I don't like it."

The boy was sitting on his bicycle and working the handbrake now.

"How far?" Hamilton said as they started down the sidewalk.

"Over in Arbuckle Court," the boy answered, and when Hamilton looked at him, the boy added, "Not far. About two blocks from here."

"What seems to be the trouble?" Hamilton asked.

"I don't know for sure. I don't understand all of it. He and Kip and this Gary Berman are supposed to have used my brother's bike while we were on vacation, and I guess they wrecked it. On purpose. But I don't know. Anyway, that's what they're talking about. My brother can't find his bike and they had it last, Kip and Roger. My mom is trying to find out where it's at."

"I know Kip," Hamilton said. "Who's this other boy?"

"Gary Berman. I guess he's new in the neighborhood. His dad is coming as soon as he gets home."

They turned a corner. The boy pushed himself along, keeping just slightly ahead. Hamilton saw an orchard, and then they turned another corner onto a dead-end street. He hadn't known of the existence of this street and was sure he would not recognize any of the people who lived here. He looked around him at the unfamiliar houses and was struck with the range of his son's personal life.

The boy turned into a driveway and got off the bicycle and leaned it against the house. When the boy opened the front door, Hamilton followed him through the living room and into the kitchen, where he saw his son sitting on one side of a table along with Kip Hollister and another boy. Hamilton looked closely at Roger and then he turned to the stout, dark-haired woman at the head of the table.

"You're Roger's father?" the woman said to him.

"Yes, my name is Evan Hamilton. Good evening."

"I'm Mrs Miller, Gilbert's mother," she said. "Sorry to ask you over here, but we have a problem."

Hamilton sat down in a chair at the other end of the table and looked around. A boy of nine or ten, the boy whose bicycle was missing, Hamilton supposed, sat next to the woman. Another boy, fourteen or so, sat on the draining board, legs dangling, and watched another boy who was talking on the telephone. Grinning slyly at something that had just been said to him over the line, the boy reached over to the sink with a cigarette. Hamilton heard the sound of the cigarette sputting out in a glass of water. The boy who had brought him leaned against the refrigerator and crossed his arms.

"Did you get one of Kip's parents?" the woman said to the boy.

"His sister said they were shopping. I went to Gary Berman's and his father will be here in a few minutes. I left the address."

"Mr Hamilton," the woman said, "I'll tell you what happened. We were on vacation last month and Kip wanted to borrow Gilbert's bike so that Roger could help him with Kip's paper route. I guess Roger's bike had a flat tire or something. Well, as it turns out —"

"Gary was choking me, Dad," Roger said.

"What?" Hamilton said, looking at his son carefully.

"He was choking me. I got the marks." His son pulled down the collar of his T-shirt to show his neck.

"They were out in the garage," the woman continued. "I didn't know what they were doing until Curt, my oldest, went out to see."

"He started it!" Gary Berman said to Hamilton. "He called me a jerk." Gary Berman looked toward the front door.

"I think my bike cost about sixty dollars, you guys," the boy named Gilbert said. "You can pay me for it."

"You keep out of this, Gilbert," the woman said to him.

Hamilton took a breath. "Go on," he said.

"Well, as it turns out, Kip and Roger used Gilbert's bike to help Kip deliver his papers, and then the two of them, and Gary too, they say, took turns rolling it."

"What do you mean 'rolling it'?" Hamilton said.

"Rolling it," the woman said. "Sending it down the street with a push and letting it fall over. Then, mind you – and they just admitted this a few minutes ago – Kip and Roger took it up to the school and threw it against a goalpost."

"Is that true, Roger?" Hamilton said, looking at his son again.

"Part of it's true, Dad," Roger said, looking down and rubbing his finger over the table. "But we only rolled it once. Kip did it, then Gary, and then I did it."

"Once is too much," Hamilton said. "Once is one too many times, Roger. I'm surprised and disappointed in you. And you too, Kip," Hamilton said.

"But you see," the woman said, "someone's fibbing tonight or else not telling all he knows, for the fact is the bike's still missing."

The older boys in the kitchen laughed and kidded with the boy who still talked on the telephone.

"We don't know where the bike is, Mrs Miller," the boy named Kip said. "We told you already. The last time we saw it was when me and Roger took it to my house after we had it at school. I mean, that was the next to last time. The very last time was when I took it back here the next morning and parked it behind the house." He shook his head. "We don't know where it is," the boy said.

"Sixty dollars," the boy named Gilbert said to the boy named Kip. "You can pay me off like five dollars a week."

"Gilbert, I'm warning you," the woman said. "You see, *they* claim," the woman went on, frowning now, "it disappeared from *here*, from behind the house. But how can we believe them when they haven't been all that truthful this evening?"

"We've told the truth," Roger said. "Everything."

Gilbert leaned back in his chair and shook his head at Hamilton's son.

The doorbell sounded and the boy on the draining board jumped down and went into the living room.

A stiff-shouldered man with a crew haircut and sharp gray eyes entered the kitchen without speaking. He glanced at the woman and moved over behind Gary Berman's chair.

"You must be Mr Berman?" the woman said. "Happy to meet you. I'm Gilbert's mother, and this is Mr Hamilton, Roger's father."

The man inclined his head at Hamilton but did not offer his hand.

"What's all this about?" Berman said to his son.

The boys at the table began to speak at once.

"Quiet down!" Berman said. "I'm talking to Gary. You'll get your turn."

The boy began his account of the affair. His father listened closely, now and then narrowing his eyes to study the other two boys.

When Gary Berman had finished, the woman said, "I'd like to get to the bottom of this. I'm not accusing any one of them, you understand, Mr Hamilton, Mr Berman – I'd just like to get to the bottom of this." She looked steadily at Roger and Kip, who were shaking their heads at Gary Berman.

"It's not true, Gary," Roger said.

"Dad, can I talk to you in private?" Gary Berman said.

"Let's go," the man said, and they walked into the living room.

Hamilton watched them go. He had the feeling he should stop them, this secrecy. His palms were wet, and he reached to his shirt pocket for a cigarette. Then, breathing deeply, he passed the back of his hand under his nose and said, "Roger, do you know any more about this, other than what you've already said? Do you know where Gilbert's bike is?"

"No, I don't," the boy said. "I swear it."

"When was the last time you saw the bicycle?" Hamilton said.

"When we brought it home from school and left it at Kip's house."

"Kip," Hamilton said, "do you know where Gilbert's bicycle is now?"

"I swear I don't, either," the boy answered. "I brought it back the next morning after we had it at school and I parked it behind the garage."

"I thought you said you left it behind the *house*," the woman said quickly.

"I mean the house! That's what I meant," the boy said.

"Did you come back here some other day to ride it?" she asked, leaning forward.

"No, I didn't," Kip answered.

"Kip?" she said.

"I didn't! I don't know where it is!" the boy shouted.

The woman raised her shoulders and let them drop. "How do you know who or what to believe?" she said to Hamilton. "All I know is, Gilbert's missing a bicycle."

* * *

Gary Berman and his father returned to the kitchen.

"It was Roger's idea to roll it," Gary Berman said.

"It was yours!" Roger said, coming out of his chair. "You wanted to! Then you wanted to take it to the orchard and strip it!"

"You shut up!" Berman said to Roger. "You can speak when spoken to, young man, not before. Gary, I'll handle this – dragged out at night because of a couple of roughnecks! Now if either of you," Berman said, looking first at Kip and then Roger, "know where this kid's bicycle is, I'd advise you to start talking."

"I think you're getting out of line," Hamilton said.

"What?" Berman said, his forehead darkening. "And I think you'd do better to mind your own business!"

"Let's go, Roger," Hamilton said, standing up. "Kip, you come now or stay." He turned to the woman. "I don't know what else we can do tonight. I intend to talk this over more with Roger, but if there is a question of restitution I feel since Roger did help manhandle the bike, he can pay a third if it comes to that."

"I don't know what to say," the woman replied, following Hamilton through the living room. "I'll talk to Gilbert's father – he's out of town now. We'll see. It's probably one of those things finally, but I'll talk to his father."

Hamilton moved to one side so that the boys could pass ahead of him onto the porch, and from behind him he heard Gary Berman say, "He called me a jerk, Dad."

"He did, did he?" Hamilton heard Berman say. "Well, he's the jerk. He looks like a jerk."

Hamilton turned and said, "I think you're seriously out of line here tonight, Mr Berman. Why don't you get control of yourself?"

"And I told you I think you should keep out of it!" Berman said.

"You get home, Roger," Hamilton said, moistening his lips. "I mean it," he said, "get going!" Roger and Kip moved out to the sidewalk. Hamilton stood in the doorway and looked at Berman, who was crossing the living room with his son.

"Mr Hamilton," the woman began nervously but did not finish.

"What do you want?" Berman said to him. "Watch out now, get out of my way!" Berman brushed Hamilton's shoulder and Hamilton stepped off the porch into some prickly cracking bushes. He couldn't believe it was happening. He moved out of the bushes and lunged at the man where he stood on the porch. They fell heavily onto the lawn. They rolled on the lawn, Hamilton wrestling Berman onto his back and coming down hard with his knees on the man's biceps. He had Berman by the collar now and began to pound his head against the lawn while the woman cried, "God almighty, someone stop them! For God's sake, someone call the police!"

Hamilton stopped.

Berman looked up at him and said, "Get off me."

"Are you all right?" the woman called to the men as they separated. "For God's sake," she said. She looked at the men, who stood a few feet apart, backs to each other, breathing hard. The older boys had crowded onto the porch to watch; now that it was over, they waited, watching the men, and then they began feinting and punching each other on the arms and ribs.

"You boys get back in the house," the woman said. "I never thought I'd see," she said and put her hand on her breast.

Hamilton was sweating and his lungs burned when he tried to take a deep breath. There was a ball of something in his throat so that he couldn't swallow for a minute. He started walking, his son and the boy named Kip at his sides. He heard car doors slam, an engine start. Headlights swept over him as he walked.

Roger sobbed once, and Hamilton put his arm around the boy's shoulders.

"I better get home," Kip said and began to cry. "My dad'll be looking for me," and the boy ran.

"I'm sorry," Hamilton said. "I'm sorry you had to see something like that," Hamilton said to his son.

They kept walking and when they reached their block, Hamilton took his arm away.

"What if he'd picked up a knife, Dad? Or a club?"

"He wouldn't have done anything like that," Hamilton said.

"But what if he had?" his son said.

"It's hard to say what people will do when they're angry," Hamilton said.

They started up the walk to their door. His heart moved when

Hamilton saw the lighted windows.

"Let me feel your muscle," his son said.

"Not now," Hamilton said. "You just go in now and have your dinner and hurry up to bed. Tell your mother I'm all right and I'm going to sit on the porch for a few minutes."

The boy rocked from one foot to the other and looked at his father, and then he dashed into the house and began calling, "Mom! Mom!"

He sat on the porch and leaned against the garage wall and stretched his legs. The sweat had dried on his forehead. He felt clammy under his clothes.

He had once seen his father – a pale, slow-talking man with slumped shoulders – in something like this. It was a bad one, and both men had been hurt. It had happened in a café. The other man was a farmhand. Hamilton had loved his father and could recall many things about him. But now he recalled his father's one fistfight as if it were all there was to the man.

He was still sitting on the porch when his wife came out.

"Dear God," she said and took his head in her hands. "Come in and shower and then have something to eat and tell me about it. Everything is still warm. Roger has gone to bed."

But he heard his son calling him.

"He's still awake," she said.

"I'll be down in a minute," Hamilton said. "Then maybe we should have a drink."

She shook her head. "I really don't believe any of this yet."

He went into the boy's room and sat down at the foot of the bed.

"It's pretty late and you're still up, so I'll say good night," Hamilton said.

"Good night," the boy said, hands behind his neck, elbows jutting.

He was in his pajamas and had a warm fresh smell about him that Hamilton breathed deeply. He patted his son through the covers.

"You take it easy from now on. Stay away from that part of the neighborhood, and don't let me ever hear of you damaging a bicycle or any other personal property. Is that clear?" Hamilton said.

The boy nodded. He took his hands from behind his neck and began picking at something on the bedspread.

"Okay, then," Hamilton said, "I'll say good night."

He moved to kiss his son, but the boy began talking.

"Dad, was Grandfather strong like you? When he was your age, I mean, you know, and you – "

"And I was nine years old? Is that what you mean? Yes, I guess he was," Hamilton said.

"Sometimes I can hardly remember him," the boy said. "I don't want to forget him or anything, you know? You know what I mean, Dad?"

When Hamilton did not answer at once, the boy went on. "When you were young, was it like it is with you and me? Did you love him more than me? Or just the same?" The boy said this abruptly. He moved his feet under the covers and looked away. When Hamilton still did not answer, the boy said, "Did he smoke? I think I remember a pipe or something."

"He started smoking a pipe before he died, that's true," Hamilton said. "He used to smoke cigarettes a long time ago and then he'd get depressed with something or other and quit, but later he'd change brands and start in again. Let me show you something," Hamilton said. "Smell the back of my hand."

The boy took the hand in his, sniffed it, and said, "I guess I don't smell anything, Dad. What is it?"

Hamilton sniffed the hand and then the fingers. "Now I can't smell anything, either," he said. "It was there before, but now it's gone." Maybe it was scared out of me, he thought. "I wanted to show you something. All right, it's late now. You better go to sleep," Hamilton said.

The boy rolled onto his side and watched his father walk to the door and watched him put his hand to the switch. And then the boy said, "Dad? You'll think I'm pretty crazy, but I wish I'd known you when you were little. I mean, about as old as I am right now. I don't know how to say it, but I'm lonesome about it. It's like – it's like I miss you already if I think about it now. That's pretty crazy, isn't it? Anyway, please leave the door open."

Hamilton left the door open, and then he thought better of it and closed it halfway.

Are These Actual Miles?

Fact is the car needs to be sold in a hurry, and Leo sends Toni out to do it. Toni is smart and has personality. She used to sell children's encyclopedias door to door. She signed him up, even though he didn't have kids. Afterward, Leo asked her for a date, and the date led to this. This deal has to be cash, and it has to be done tonight. Tomorrow somebody they owe might slap a lien on the car. Monday they'll be in court, home free – but word on them went out yesterday, when their lawyer mailed the letters of intention. The hearing on Monday is nothing to worry about, the lawyer has said. They'll be asked some questions, and they'll sign some papers, and that's it. But sell the convertible, he said – today, *tonight*. They can hold onto the little car, Leo's car, no problem. But they go into court with that big convertible, the court will take it, and that's that.

Toni dresses up. It's four o'clock in the afternoon. Leo worries the lots will close. But Toni takes her time dressing. She puts on a new white blouse, wide lacy cuffs, the new two-piece suit, new heels. She transfers the stuff from her straw purse into the new patent-leather handbag. She studies the lizard makeup pouch and puts that in too. Toni has been two hours on her hair and face. Leo stands in the bedroom doorway and taps his lips with his knuckles, watching.

"You're making me nervous," she says. "I wish you wouldn't just stand," she says. "So tell me how I look."

"You look fine," he says. "You look great. I'd buy a car from you anytime."

"But you don't have money," she says, peering into the mirror. She pats her hair, frowns. "And your credit's lousy. You're nothing," she says. "Teasing," she says and looks at him in the mirror. "Don't be serious," she says. "It has to be done, so I'll do it. You take it out, you'd be lucky to get three, four hundred and we both know it. Honey, you'd be lucky if you didn't have to pay *them*." She gives her hair a final pat, gums her lips, blots the lipstick with a tissue. She turns away from the mirror and picks up her purse. "I'll have to have dinner or something, I told you that already, that's the way they work, I know them. But don't worry, I'll get out of it," she says. "I can handle it."

"Jesus," Leo says, "did you have to say that?"

She looks at him steadily. "Wish me luck," she says.

"Luck," he says. "You have the pink slip?" he says.

She nods. He follows her through the house, a tall woman with a small high bust, broad hips and thighs. He scratches a pimple on his neck. "You're sure?" he says. "Make sure. You have to have the pink slip."

"I have the pink slip," she says.

"Make sure."

She starts to say something, instead looks at herself in the front window and then shakes her head.

"At least call," he says. "Let me know what's going on."

"I'll call," she says. "Kiss, kiss. Here," she says and points to the corner of her mouth. "Careful," she says.

He holds the door for her. "Where are you going to try first?" he says. She moves past him and onto the porch.

Ernest Williams looks from across the street. In his Bermuda shorts, stomach hanging, he looks at Leo and Toni as he directs a spray onto his begonias. Once, last winter, during the holidays, when Toni and the kids were visiting his mother's, Leo brought a woman home. Nine o'clock the next morning, a cold foggy Saturday, Leo walked the woman to the car, surprised Ernest Williams on the sidewalk with a newspaper in his hand. Fog drifted, Ernest Williams stared, then slapped the paper against his leg, hard.

Leo recalls that slap, hunches his shoulders, says, "You have someplace in mind first?"

"I'll just go down the line," she says. "The first lot, then I'll just go down the line."

"Open at nine hundred," he says. "Then come down. Nine hundred is low bluebook, even on a cash deal."

"I know where to start," she says.

Ernest Williams turns the hose in their direction. He stares at them through the spray of water. Leo has an urge to cry out a confession.

"Just making sure," he says.

"Okay, okay," she says. "I'm off."

It's her car, they call it her car, and that makes it all the worse. They bought it new that summer three years ago. She wanted something to do after the kids started school, so she went back selling. He was working six days a week in the fiber-glass plant. For a while they didn't know how to spend the money. Then they put a thousand on the convertible and doubled and tripled the payments until in a year they had it paid. Earlier, while she was dressing, he took the jack and spare from the trunk and emptied the glove compartment of pencils, matchbooks, Blue Chip stamps. Then he washed it and vacuumed inside. The red hood and fenders shine.

"Good luck," he says and touches her elbow.

She nods. He sees she is already gone, already negotiating.

"Things are going to be different!" he calls to her as she reaches the driveway. "We start over Monday. I mean it."

Ernest Williams looks at them and turns his head and spits. She gets into the car and lights a cigarette.

"This time next week!" Leo calls again. "Ancient history!"

He waves as she backs into the street. She changes gear and starts ahead. She accelerates and the tires give a little scream.

In the kitchen Leo pours Scotch and carries the drink to the backyard. The kids are at his mother's. There was a letter three days ago, his name penciled on the outside of the dirty envelope, the only letter all summer not demanding payment in full. We are having fun, the letter said. We like Grandma. We have a new dog called Mr Six. He is nice. We love him. Goodbye.

He goes for another drink. He adds ice and sees that his hand trembles. He holds the hand over the sink. He looks at the hand for a while, sets down the glass, and holds out the other hand. Then he picks up the glass and goes back outside to sit on the steps. He recalls when he was a kid his dad pointing at a fine house, a tall white house surrounded by apple trees and a high white rail fence. "That's Finch," his dad said admiringly. "He's been in bankruptcy at least twice. Look at that house." But bankruptcy is a company collapsing utterly, executives cutting their wrists and throwing themselves from windows, thousands of men on the street.

Leo and Toni still had furniture. Leo and Toni had furniture and Toni and the kids had clothes. Those things were exempt. What else? Bicycles for the kids, but these he had sent to his mother's for safekeeping. The portable air-conditioner and the appliances, new washer and dryer, trucks came for those things weeks ago. What else did they have? This and that, nothing mainly, stuff that wore out or fell to pieces long ago. But there were some big parties back there, some fine travel. To Reno and Tahoe, at eighty with the top down and the radio playing. Food, that was one of the big items. They gorged on food. He figures thousands on luxury items alone. Toni would go to the grocery and put in everything she saw. "I had to do without when I was a kid," she says. "These kids are not going to do without," as if he'd been insisting they should. She joins all the book clubs. "We never had books around when I was a kid," she says as she tears open the heavy packages. They enroll in the record clubs for something to play on the new stereo. They sign up for it all. Even a pedigreed terrier named Ginger. He paid two hundred and found her run over in the street a week later. They buy what they want. If they can't pay, they charge. They sign up.

His undershirt is wet; he can feel the sweat rolling from his underarms. He sits on the step with the empty glass in his hand and watches the shadows fill up the yard. He stretches, wipes his face. He listens to the traffic on the highway and considers whether he should go to the base-ment, stand on the utility sink, and hang himself with his belt. He under-stands he is willing to be dead.

Inside he makes a large drink and he turns the TV on and he fixes some-thing to eat. He sits at the table with chili and crackers and watches something about a blind detective. He clears the table. He washes the pan and the bowl, dries these things and puts them away, then allows himself a look at the clock.

It's after nine. She's been gone nearly five hours.

He pours Scotch, adds water, carries the drink to the living room. He sits on the couch but finds his shoulders so stiff they won't let him lean back. He stares at the screen and sips, and soon he goes for another drink. He sits again. A news program begins – it's ten o'clock – and he says, "God, what in God's name has gone wrong?" and goes to the kitchen to return with more Scotch. He sits, he closes his eyes, and opens them when he hears the telephone ringing.

"I wanted to call," she says.

"Where are you?" he says. He hears piano music, and his heart moves. "I don't know," she says. "Someplace. We're having a drink, then we're going someplace else for dinner. I'm with the sales manager. He's crude, but he's all right. He bought the car. I have to go now. I was on my way to the ladies and saw the phone."

"Did somebody buy the car?" Leo says. He looks out the kitchen window to the place in the drive where she always parks.

"I told you," she says. "I have to go now."

"Wait, wait a minute, for Christ's sake," he says. "Did somebody buy the car or not?"

"He had his checkbook out when I left," she says. "I have to go now. I have to go to the bathroom."

"Wait!" he yells. The line goes dead. He listens to the dial tone. "Jesus Christ," he says as he stands with the receiver in his hand.

He circles the kitchen and goes back to the living room. He sits. He gets up. In the bathroom he brushes his teeth very carefully. Then he uses dental floss. He washes his face and goes back to the kitchen. He looks at the clock and takes a clean glass from a set that has a hand of playing cards painted on each glass. He fills the glass with ice. He stares for a while at the glass he left in the sink.

He sits against one end of the couch and puts his legs up at the other end. He looks at the screen, realizes he can't make out what the people are saying. He turns the empty glass in his hand and considers biting off the rim. He shivers for a time and thinks of going to bed, though he knows he will dream of a large woman with gray hair. In the dream he is always leaning over tying his shoelaces. When he straightens up, she looks at him, and he bends to tie again. He looks at his hand. It makes a fist as he watches. The telephone is ringing.

"Where are you, honey?" he says slowly, gently.

"We're at this restaurant," she says, her voice strong, bright.

"Honey, which restaurant?" he says. He puts the heel of his hand against his eye and pushes.

"Downtown someplace," she says. "I think it's New Jimmy's. Excuse me," she says to someone off the line, "is this place New Jimmy's? This is New Jimmy's, Leo," she says to him. "Everything is all right, we're almost finished, then he's going to bring me home."

"Honey?" he says. He holds the receiver against his ear and rocks back and forth, eyes closed. "Honey?"

"I have to go," she says. "I wanted to call. Anyway, guess how much?"

"Honey," he says.

"Six and a quarter," she says. "I have it in my purse. He said there's no market for convertibles. I guess we're born lucky," she says and laughs. "I told him everything. I think I had to."

"Honey," Leo says.

"What?" she says.

"Please, honey," Leo says.

"He said he sympathizes," she says. "But he would have said anything." She laughs again. "He said personally he'd rather be classified a robber or a rapist than a bankrupt. He's nice enough, though," she says.

"Come home," Leo says. "Take a cab and come home."

"I can't," she says. "I told you, we're halfway through dinner."

"I'll come for you," he says.

"No," she says. "I said we're just finishing. I told you, it's part of the deal. They're out for all they can get. But don't worry, we're about to leave. I'll be home in a little while." She hangs up.

In a few minutes he calls New Jimmy's. A man answers. "New Jimmy's has closed for the evening," the man says.

"I'd like to talk to my wife," Leo says.

"Does she work here?" the man asks. "Who is she?"

"She's a customer," Leo says. "She's with someone. A business person."

"Would I know her?" the man says. "What is her name?"

"I don't think you know her," Leo says.

"That's all right," Leo says. "That's all right. I see her now."

"Thank you for calling New Jimmy's," the man says.

Leo hurries to the window. A car he doesn't recognize slows in front of the house, then picks up speed. He waits. Two, three hours later, the telephone rings again. There is no one at the other end when he picks up the receiver. There is only a dial tone.

"I'm right here!" Leo screams into the receiver.

Near dawn he hears footsteps on the porch. He gets up from the couch. The set hums, the screen glows. He opens the door. She bumps the wall coming in. She grins. Her face is puffy, as if she's been sleeping under sedation. She works her lips, ducks heavily and sways as he cocks his fist.

"Go ahead," she says thickly. She stands there swaying. Then she makes a noise and lunges, catches his shirt, tears it down the front. "Bankrupt!" she screams. She twists loose, grabs and tears his undershirt at the neck. "You son of a bitch," she says, clawing.

He squeezes her wrists, then lets go, steps back, looking for something heavy. She stumbles as she heads for the bedroom. "Bankrupt," she mutters. He hears her fall on the bed and groan.

He waits awhile, then splashes water on his face and goes to the bedroom. He turns the lights on, looks at her, and begins to take her clothes off. He pulls and pushes her from side to side undressing her. She says something in her sleep and moves her hand. He takes off her underpants, looks at them closely under the light, and throws them into a corner. He turns back the covers and rolls her in, naked. Then he opens her purse. He is reading the check when he hears the car come into the drive.

He looks through the front curtain and sees the convertible in the drive, its motor running smoothly, the headlamps burning, and he closes and opens his eyes. He sees a tall man come around in front of the car and up to the front porch. The man lays something on the porch and starts back to the car. He wears a white linen suit.

Leo turns on the porch light and opens the door cautiously. Her makeup pouch lies on the top step. The man looks at Leo across the front of the car, and then gets back inside and releases the handbrake.

"Wait!" Leo calls and starts down the steps. The man brakes the car as Leo walks in front of the lights. The car creaks against the brake. Leo tries to pull the two pieces of his shirt together, tries to bunch it all into his trousers.

"What is it you want?" the man says. "Look," the man says, "I have to go. No offense. I buy and sell cars, right? The lady left her makeup. She's a fine lady, very refined. What is it?"

Leo leans against the door and looks at the man. The man takes his hands off the wheel and puts them back. He drops the gear into reverse and the car moves backward a little.

"I want to tell you," Leo says and wets his lips.

The light in Ernest Williams' bedroom goes on. The shade rolls up.

Leo shakes his head, tucks in his shirt again. He steps back from the car. "Monday," he says.

"Monday," the man says and watches for sudden movement.

Leo nods slowly.

"Well, goodnight," the man says and coughs. "Take it easy, hear? Monday, that's right. Okay, then." He takes his foot off the brake, puts it on again after he has rolled back two or three feet. "Hey, one question. Between friends, are these actual miles?" The man waits, then clears his throat. "Okay, look, it doesn't matter either way," the man says. "I have to go. Take it easy." He backs into the street, pulls away quickly, and turns the corner without stopping.

Leo tucks at his shirt and goes back in the house. He locks the front door and checks it. Then he goes to the bedroom and locks that door and turns back the covers. He looks at her before he flicks the light. He takes off his clothes, folds them carefully on the floor, and gets in beside her. He lies on his back for a time and pulls the hair on his stomach, considering. He looks at the bedroom door, outlined now in the faint outside light. Presently he reaches out his hand and touches her hip. She does not move. He turns on his side and puts his hand on her hip. He runs his fingers over her hip and feels the stretch marks there. They are like roads, and he traces them in her flesh. He runs his fingers back and forth, first one, then another. They run everywhere in her flesh, dozens, perhaps hundreds of them. He remembers waking up the morning after they bought the car, seeing it, there in the drive, in the sun, gleaming.

Signals

As their first of the extravagances they had planned for that evening, Wayne and Caroline went to Aldo's, an elegant new restaurant north a good distance. They passed through a tiny walled garden with small pieces of statuary and were met by a tall graying man in a dark suit who said, "Good evening, sir. Madam," and who swung open the heavy door for them.

Inside, Aldo himself showed them the aviary – a peacock, a pair of golden pheasants, a Chinese ring-necked pheasant, and a number of unannounced birds that flew around or sat perched. Aldo personally conducted them to a table, seated Caroline, and then turned to Wayne and said, "A lovely lady," before moving off – a dark, small, impeccable man with a soft accent.

They were pleased with his attention.

"I read in the paper," Wayne said, "that he has an uncle who has some kind of position in the Vatican. That's how he was able to get copies of some of these paintings." Wayne nodded at a Velasquez reproduction on the nearest wall. "His uncle in the Vatican," Wayne said.

"He used to be *maître d'* at the Copacabana in Rio," Caroline said. "He knew Frank Sinatra, and Lana Turner was a good friend of his."

"Is that so?" Wayne said. "I didn't know that. I read that he was at the Victoria Hotel in Switzerland and at some big hotel in Paris. I didn't know he was at the Copacabana in Rio."

Caroline moved her handbag slightly as the waiter set down the heavy goblets. He poured water and then moved to Wayne's side of the table.

"Did you see the suit he was wearing?" Wayne said. "You seldom see a suit like that. That's a three-hundred-dollar suit." He picked up his menu. In a while, he said, "Well, what are you going to have?"

"I don't know," she said. "I haven't decided. What are you going to have?"

"I don't know," he said. "I haven't decided, either."

"What about one of these French dishes, Wayne? Or else this? Over here on this side." She placed her finger in instruction, and then she narrowed her eyes at him as he located the language, pursed his lips, frowned, and shook his head.

"I don't know," he said. "I'd kind of like to know what I'm getting. I just don't really know."

The waiter returned with card and pencil and said something Wayne couldn't quite catch.

"We haven't decided yet," Wayne said. He shook his head as the waiter continued to stand beside the table. "I'll signal you when we're ready."

"I think I'll just have a sirloin. You order what you want," he said to Caroline when the waiter had moved off. He closed the menu and raised his goblet. Over the muted voices coming from the other tables Wayne could hear a warbling call from the aviary. He saw Aldo greet a party of four, chat with them as he smiled and nodded and led them to a table.

"We could have had a better table," Wayne said. "Instead of right here in the center where everyone can walk by and watch you eat. We could have had a table against the wall. Or over there by the fountain."

"I think I'll have the beef Tournedos," Caroline said.

She kept looking at her menu. He tapped out a cigarette, lighted it, and then glanced around at the other diners. Caroline still stared at her menu.

"Well, for God's sake, if that's what you're going to have, close your menu so he can take our order." Wayne raised his arm for the waiter, who lingered near the back talking with another waiter.

"Nothing else to do but gas around with the other waiters," Wayne said.

"He's coming," Caroline said.

"Sir?" The waiter was a thin pock-faced man in a loose black suit and a black bow tie.

". . . And we'll have a bottle of champagne, I believe. A small bottle. Something, you know, domestic," Wayne said.

"Yes, sir," the waiter said.

"And we'll have that right away. Before the salad or the relish plate," Wayne said.

"Oh, bring the relish *tray*, anyway," Caroline said. "Please."

"Yes, madam," the waiter said.

"They're a slippery bunch," Wayne said. "Do you remember that guy named Bruno who used to work at the office during the week and wait tables on weekends? Fred caught him stealing out of the petty-cash box. We fired him."

"Let's talk about something pleasant," Caroline said.

"All right, sure," Wayne said.

The waiter poured a little champagne into Wayne's glass, and Wayne took the glass, tasted, and said, "Fine, that will do nicely." Then he said, "Here's to you, baby," and raised his glass high. "Happy birthday."

They clinked glasses.

"I like champagne," Caroline said.

"I like champagne," Wayne said.

"We could have had a bottle of Lancer's," Caroline said.

"Well, why didn't you say something, if that's what you wanted?" Wayne said.

"I don't know," Caroline said. "I just didn't think about it. This is fine, though."

"I don't know too much about champagnes. I don't mind admitting I'm not much of a . . . connoisseur. I don't mind admitting I'm just a lowbrow." He laughed and tried to catch her eye, but she was busy selecting an olive from the relish dish. "Not like the group you've been keeping company with lately. But if you wanted Lancer's," he went on, "you should have ordered Lancer's."

"Oh, shut up!" she said. "Can't you talk about something else?" She looked up at him then and he had to look away. He moved his feet under the table.

He said, "Would you care for some more champagne, dear?"

"Yes, thank you," she said quietly.

"Here's to us," he said.

"To us, my darling," she said.

They looked steadily at each other as they drank.

"We ought to do this more often," he said.

She nodded.

"It's good to get out now and then. I'll make more of an effort, if you want me to."

She reached for celery. "That's up to you."

"That's not true! It's not me who's . . . who's . . ."

"Who's what?" she said.

"I don't care what you do," he said, dropping his eyes.

"Is that true?"

"I don't know why I said that," he said.

The waiter brought the soup and took away the bottle and the wineglasses and refilled their goblets with water.

"Could I have a soup spoon?" Wayne asked.

"Sir?"

"A soup spoon," Wayne repeated.

The waiter looked amazed and then perplexed. He glanced around at the other tables. Wayne made a shoveling motion over his soup. Aldo appeared beside the table.

"Is everything all right? Is there anything wrong?"

"My husband doesn't seem to have a soup spoon," Caroline said. "I'm sorry for the disturbance," she said.

"Certainly. *Une cuiller, s'il vous plaît*," Aldo said to the waiter in an even voice. He looked once at Wayne and then explained to Caroline. "This is Paul's first night. He speaks little English, yet I trust you will agree he is an excellent waiter. The boy who set the table forgot the spoon." Aldo smiled. "It no doubt took Paul by surprise."

"This is a beautiful place," Caroline said.

"Thank you," Aldo said. "I'm delighted you could come tonight. Would you like to see the wine cellar and the private dining rooms?"

"Very much," Caroline said.

"I will have someone show you around when you have finished dining," Aldo said.

"We'll be looking forward to it," Caroline said.

Aldo bowed slightly and looked again at Wayne. "I hope you enjoy your dinner," he said to them.

"That jerk," Wayne said.

"Who?" she said. "Who are you talking about?" she said, laying down her spoon.

"The waiter," Wayne said. "The waiter. The newest and the dumbest waiter in the house, and we got him."

"Eat your soup," she said. "Don't blow a gasket."

Wayne lighted a cigarette. The waiter arrived with salads and took away the soup bowls.

When they had started on the main course, Wayne said, "Well, what do you think? Is there a chance for us or not?" He looked down and arranged the napkin on his lap.

"Maybe so," she said. "There's always a chance."

"Don't give me that kind of crap," he said. "Answer me straight for a change."

"Don't snap at me," she said.

"I'm asking you," he said. "Give me a straight answer," he said.

She said, "You want something signed in blood?"

He said, "That wouldn't be such a bad idea."

She said, "You listen to me! I've given you the best years of my life. The best years of my life!"

"The best years of *your* life?" he said.

"I'm thirty-six years old," she said. "Thirty-seven to night. Tonight, right now, at this minute, I just can't say what I'm going to do. I'll just have to see," she said.

"I don't care what you do," he said.

"Is that true?" she said.

He threw down his fork and tossed his napkin on the table.

"Are you finished?" she asked pleasantly. "Let's have coffee and dessert. We'll have a nice dessert. Something good."

She finished everything on her plate.

"Two coffees," Wayne said to the waiter. He looked at her and then back to the waiter. "What do you have for dessert?" he said.

"Sir?" the waiter said.

"Dessert!" Wayne said.

The waiter gazed at Caroline and then at Wayne.

"No dessert," she said. "Let's not have any dessert."

"Chocolate mousse," the waiter said. "Orange sherbet," the waiter said. He smiled, showing his bad teeth. "Sir?"

"And I don't want any guided tour of this place," Wayne said when the waiter had moved off.

When they rose from the table, Wayne dropped a dollar bill near his coffee cup. Caroline took two dollars from her handbag, smoothed the bills out, and placed them alongside the other dollar, the three bills lined up in a row.

She waited with Wayne while he paid the check. Out of the corner of his eye, Wayne could see Aldo standing near the door dropping grains of seed into the aviary. Aldo looked in their direction, smiled, and went on rubbing the seeds from between his fingers as birds collected in front of him. Then he briskly brushed his hands together and started moving toward Wayne, who looked away, who turned slightly but significantly as Aldo neared him. But when Wayne looked back, he saw Aldo take Caroline's waiting hand, saw Aldo draw his heels smartly together, saw Aldo kiss her wrist.

"Did madam enjoy her dinner?" Aldo said.

"It was marvelous," Caroline said.

"You will come back from time to time?" Aldo said.

"I shall," Caroline said. "As often as I may. Next time, I should like to have your permission to check things out a little, but this time we simply must go."

"Dear lady," Aldo said. "I have something for you. One moment, please." He reached to a vase on a table near the door and swung gracefully back with a long-stemmed rose.

"For you, dear lady," Aldo said. "But caution, please. The thorns. A very lovely lady," he said to Wayne and smiled at him and turned to welcome another couple.

Caroline stood there.

"Let's get out of here," Wayne said.

"You can see how he could be friends with Lana Turner," Caroline said. She held the rose and turned it between her fingers.

"Good night!" she called out to Aldo's back.

But Aldo was occupied selecting another rose.

"I don't think he ever knew her," Wayne said.

Will You Please Be Quiet, Please?

I

When he was eighteen and was leaving home for the first time, Ralph Wyman was counseled by his father, principal of Jefferson Elementary School and trumpet soloist in the Weaverville Elks Club Auxiliary Band, that life was a very serious matter, an enterprise insisting on strength and purpose in a young person just setting out, an arduous undertaking, everyone knew that, but nevertheless a rewarding one, Ralph Wyman's father believed and said.

But in college Ralph's goals were hazy. He thought he wanted to be a doctor and he thought he wanted to be lawyer, and he took pre-medical courses and courses in the history of jurisprudence and business law before he decided he had neither the emotional detachment necessary for medicine nor the ability for sustained reading required in law, especially as such reading might concern property and inheritance. Though he continued to take classes here and there in the sciences and in business, Ralph also took some classes in philosophy and literature and felt himself on the brink of some kind of huge discovery about himself. But it never came. It was during this time – his lowest ebb, as he referred to it later – that Ralph believed he almost had a breakdown; he was in a fraternity and he got drunk every night. He drank so much that he acquired a reputation and was called "Jackson", after the bartender at The Keg.

Then, in his third year, Ralph came under the influence of a particularly persuasive teacher. Dr Maxwell was his name; Ralph would never forget him. He was a handsome, graceful man in his early forties, with exquisite manners and with just the trace of the South in his voice. He had been educated at Vanderbilt, had studied in Europe, and had later had something to do with one or two literary magazines back East. Almost overnight, Ralph would later say, he decided on teaching as a career.

He stopped drinking quite so much, began to bear down on his studies, and within a year was elected to Omega Psi, the national journalism fraternity; he became a member of the English Club; was invited to come with his cello, which he hadn't played in three years, and join in a student chamber-music group just forming; and he even ran successfully for secretary of the senior class. It was then that he met Marian Ross – a handsomely pale and slender girl who took a seat beside him in a Chaucer class.

Marian Ross wore her hair long and favored high-necked sweaters and always went around with a leather purse on a long strap swinging from her shoulder. Her eyes were large and seemed to take in everything at a glance. Ralph liked going out with Marian Ross. They went to The Keg and to a few other spots where everyone went, but they never let their going together or their subsequent engagement the next summer interfere with their studies. They were solemn students, and both sets of parents eventually gave approval to the match. Ralph and Marian did their student teaching at the same high school in Chico in the spring and went through graduation exercises together in June. They married in St James Episcopal Church two weeks later.

They had held hands the night before their wedding and pledged to preserve forever the excitement and the mystery of marriage.

For their honeymoon they drove to Guadalajara, and while they both enjoyed visiting the decayed churches and the poorly lighted museums and the afternoons they spent shopping and exploring in the marketplace, Ralph was secretly appalled by the squalor and open lust he saw and was anxious to return to the safety of California. But the one vision he would always remember and which disturbed him most of all had nothing to do with Mexico. It was late afternoon, almost evening, and Marian was leaning motionless on her arms over the ironwork balustrade of their rented *casita* as Ralph came up the dusty road below. Her hair was long and hung down in front over her shoulders, and she was looking away from him, staring at something in the distance. She wore a white blouse with a bright red scarf at her throat, and he could see her breasts pushing against the white cloth. He had a bottle of dark, unlabeled wine under his arm, and the whole incident put Ralph in mind of something from a film, an intensely dramatic moment into which Marian could be fitted but he could not.

Before they left for their honeymoon they had accepted positions at a high school in Eureka, a town in the lumbering region in the northern part of the state. After a year, when they were sure the school and the town were exactly what they wanted to settle down to, they made a payment on a house in the Fire Hill district. Ralph felt, without really thinking about it, that he and Marian understood each other perfectly – as well, at least, as any two people might. Moreover, Ralph felt he understood himself – what he could do, what he could not do, and where he was headed with the prudent measure of himself that he made.

Their two children, Dorothea and Robert, were now five and four years old. A few months after Robert was born, Marian was offered a post as a French and English instructor at the junior college at the edge of town, and Ralph had stayed on at the high school. They considered themselves a happy couple, with only a single injury to their marriage, and that was well in the past, two years ago this winter. It was something they had never talked about since. But Ralph thought about it sometimes – indeed, he was willing to admit he thought about it more and more. Increasingly, ghastly images would be projected on his eyes, certain unthinkable particularities. For he had taken it into his head that his wife had once betrayed him with a man named Mitchell Anderson.

But now it was a Sunday night in November and the children were asleep and Ralph was sleepy and he sat on the couch grading papers and could hear the radio playing softly in the kitchen, where Marian was ironing, and he felt enormously happy. He stared a while longer at the papers in front of him, then gathered them all up and turned off the lamp.

"Finished, love?" Marian said with a smile when he appeared in the doorway. She was sitting on a tall stool, and she stood the iron up on its end as if she had been waiting for him.

"Damn it, no," he said with an exaggerated grimace, tossing the papers on the kitchen table.

She laughed – bright, pleasant – and held up her face to be kissed, and he gave her a little peck on the cheek. He pulled out a chair from the table and sat down, leaned back on the legs and looked at her. She smiled again and then lowered her eyes.

"I'm already half asleep," he said.

"Coffee?" she said, reaching over and laying the back of her hand against the percolator.

He shook his head.

She took up the cigarette she had burning in the ashtray, smoked it while she stared at the floor, and then put it back in the ashtray. She looked at him, and a warm expression moved across her face. She was tall and limber, with a good bust, narrow hips, and wide wonderful eyes.

"Do you ever think about that party?" she asked, still looking at him.

He was stunned and shifted in the chair, and he said, "Which party? You mean the one two or three years ago?"

She nodded.

He waited, and when she offered no further comment, he said, "What about it? Now that you brought it up, what about it?" Then: "He kissed you, after all, that night, didn't he? I mean, I knew he did. He did try to kiss you, or didn't he?"

"I was just thinking about it and I asked you, that's all," she said. "Sometimes I think about it," she said.

"Well, he did, didn't he? Come on, Marian," he said.

"Do you ever think about that night?" she said.

He said, "Not really. It was a long time ago, wasn't it? Three or four years ago. You can tell me now," he said. "This is still old Jackson you're talking to, remember?" And they both laughed abruptly together and abruptly she said, "Yes." She said, "He did kiss me a few times." She smiled.

He knew he should try to match her smile, but he could not. He said, "You told me before he didn't. You said he only put his arm around you while he was driving. So which is it?"

"What did you do that for?" she was saying dreamily. "Where were you all night?" he was screaming, standing over her, legs watery, fist drawn back to hit again. Then she said, "I didn't do anything. Why did you hit me?" she said.

"How did we ever get onto this?" she said.

"You brought it up," he said.

She shook her head. "I don't know what made me think of it." She pulled in her upper lip and stared at the floor. Then she straightened her shoulders and looked up. "If you'll move this ironing board for me, love, I'll make us a hot drink. A buttered rum. How does that sound?"

"Good," he said.

She went into the living room and turned on the lamp and bent to pick up a magazine from the floor. He watched her hips under the plaid woolen skirt. She moved in front of the window and stood looking out at the streetlight. She smoothed her palm down over her skirt, then began tucking in her blouse. He wondered if she wondered if he were watching her.

After he stood the ironing board in its alcove on the porch, he sat down again and, when she came into the kitchen, he said, "Well, what else went on between you and Mitchell Anderson that night?"

"Nothing," she said. "I was thinking about something else."

"What?"

"About the children, the dress I want Dorothea to have for next Easter. And about the class I'm going to have tomorrow. I was thinking of seeing how they'd go for a little Rimbaud," and she laughed. "I didn't mean to rhyme – really, Ralph, and really, nothing else happened. I'm sorry I ever said anything about it."

"Okay," he said.

He stood up and leaned against the wall by the refrigerator and watched her as she spooned out sugar into two cups and then stirred in the rum. The water was beginning to boil.

"Look, honey, it *has* been brought up now," he said, "and it *was* four years ago, so there's no reason at all I can think of that we *can't* talk about it now if we *want* to. Is there?"

She said, "There's really nothing to talk about."

He said, "I'd like to know."

She said, "Know what?"

"Whatever else he did besides kiss you. We're adults. We haven't seen the Andersons in literally years and we'll probably never see them again and it happened a *long* time ago, so what reason could there possibly be that we can't talk about it?" He was a little surprised at the reasoning quality in his voice. He sat down and looked at the tablecloth and then looked up at her again. "Well?" he said.

"Well," she said, with an impish grin, tilting her head to one side girlishly, remembering. "No, Ralph, really. I'd really just rather not."

"For Christ's sake, Marian! *Now* I mean it," he said, and he suddenly understood that he did.

She turned off the gas under the water and put her hands out on the stool; then she sat down again, hooking her heels over the bottom step. She sat forward, resting her arms across her knees, her breasts pushing at her blouse. She picked at something on her skirt and then looked up.

"You remember Emily'd already gone home with the Beattys, and for some reason Mitchell had stayed on. He looked a little out of sorts that night, to begin with. I don't know, maybe they weren't getting along, Emily and him, but I don't know that. And there were you and I, the Franklins, and Mitchell Anderson still there. All of us a little drunk. I'm not sure how it happened, Ralph, but Mitchell and I just happened to find ourselves alone together in the kitchen for a minute, and there was no whiskey left, only a part of a bottle of that white wine we had. It must've been close to one o'clock, because Mitchell said, 'If we ride on giant wings we can make it before the liquor store closes.' You know how he could be so theatrical when he wanted? Soft-shoe stuff, facial expressions? Anyway, he was very witty about it all. At least it seemed that way at the time. And very drunk, too, I might add. So was I, for that matter. It was an impulse, Ralph. I don't know why I did it, don't ask me, but when he said let's go – I agreed. We went out the back, where his car was parked. We went just as . . . we were . . . didn't even get our coats out of the closet, thought we'd just be gone a few minutes. I don't know what we thought, I thought, I don't know *why* I went, Ralph. It was an impulse, that's all I can say. It was the wrong impulse." She paused. "It was my fault that night, Ralph, and I'm sorry. I shouldn't have done anything like that – I *know* that."

"Christ!" The word leaped out of him. "But you've always been that way, Marian!" And he knew at once that he had uttered a new and profound truth.

His mind filled with a swarm of accusations, and he tried to focus on one in particular. He looked down at his hands and noticed they had the same lifeless feeling they had had when he had seen her on the balcony. He picked up the red grading pencil lying on the table and then he put it down again.

"I'm listening," he said.

"Listening to what?" she said. "You're swearing and getting upset, Ralph. For nothing – nothing, honey! . . . there's nothing *else*," she said.

"Go on," he said.

She said, "*What* is the matter with us, anyway? Do you know how this started? Because I don't know how this started."

He said, "Go on, Marian."

"That's *all*, Ralph," she said. "I've told you. We went for a ride. We talked. He kissed me. I still don't see how we could've been gone three hours – or whatever it was you said we were."

"Tell me, Marian," he said, and he knew there was more and knew he had always known. He felt a fluttering in his stomach, and then he said, "No. If you don't want to tell me, that's all right. Actually, I guess I'd just as soon leave it at that," he said. He thought fleetingly that he would be someplace else tonight doing something else, that it would be silent somewhere if he had not married.

"Ralph," she said, "you won't be angry, will you? Ralph? We're just talking. You won't, will you?" She had moved over to a chair at the table.

He said, "I won't."

She said, "Promise?"

He said, "Promise."

She lit a cigarette. He had suddenly a great desire to see the children, to get them up and out of bed, heavy and turning in their sleep, and to hold each of them on a knee, to jog them until they woke up. He moved all his attention into one of the tiny black coaches in the tablecloth. Four tiny white prancing horses pulled each one of the black coaches and the figure driving the horses had his arms up and wore a tall hat, and suitcases were strapped down atop the coach, and what looked like a kerosene lamp hung from the side, and if he were listening at all it was from inside the black coach.

"... We went straight to the liquor store, and I waited in the car until he came out. He had a sack in one hand and one of those plastic bags of ice in the other. He weaved a little getting into the car. I hadn't realized he was so drunk until we started driving again. I noticed the way he was driving. It was terribly slow. He was all hunched over the wheel. His eyes staring. We were talking about a lot of things that didn't make sense. I can't remember. We were talking about Nietzsche. Strindberg. He was directing *Miss Julie* second semester. And then something about Norman Mailer stabbing his wife in the breast. And then he stopped for a minute in the middle of the road. And we each took a drink out of the bottle. He said he'd hate to think of me being stabbed in the breast. He said he'd like to kiss my breast. He drove the car off the road. He put his head on my lap . . ."

She hurried on, and he sat with his hands folded on the table and watched her lips. His eyes skipped around the kitchen – stove, napkin-holder, stove, cupboards, toaster, back to her lips, back to the coach in the tablecloth. He felt a peculiar desire for her flicker through his groin, and then he felt the steady rocking of the coach and he wanted to call *stop* and then he heard her say, "He said shall we have a go at it?" And then she was saying, "I'm to blame. I'm the one to blame. He said he'd leave it all up to me, I could do whatever I want."

He shut his eyes. He shook his head, tried to create possibilities, other conclusions. He actually wondered if he could restore that night two years ago and imagined himself coming into the kitchen just as they were at the door, heard himself telling her in a hearty voice, oh no, no, you're not going out for anything with that Mitchell Anderson! The fellow is drunk and he's a bad driver to boot and you have to go to bed now and get up with little Robert and Dorothea in the morning and stop! Thou shalt stop!

He opened his eyes. She had a hand up over her face and was crying noisily.

"Why did you, Marian?" he asked.

She shook her head without looking up.

Then suddenly he knew! His mind buckled. For a minute he could only stare dumbly at his hands. He knew! His mind roared with the knowing.

"Christ! No! Marian! *Jesus Christ!*" he said, springing back from the table. "Christ! *No*, Marian!"

"No, no," she said, throwing her head back.

"You let him!" he screamed.

"No, no," she pleaded.

"You let him! A go at it! Didn't you? Didn't you? A *go* at it! Is that what he said? Answer me!" he screamed. "Did he come in you? Did you let him come in you when you were having your go at it?"

"Listen, listen to me, Ralph," she whimpered, "I swear to you he didn't. He didn't come. He didn't come in me." She rocked from side to side in the chair.

"Oh God! God *damn* you!" he shrieked.

"God!" she said, getting up, holding out her hands. "Are we crazy,

Ralph? Have we lost our minds? Ralph? Forgive me, Ralph. Forgive – "

"Don't touch me! Get away from me!" he screamed. He was screaming. She began to pant in her fright. She tried to head him off. But he took her by the shoulder and pushed her out of the way.

"Forgive me, Ralph! *Please.* Ralph!" she screamed.

II

He had to stop and lean against a car before going on. Two couples in evening clothes were coming down the sidewalk toward him, and one of the men was telling a story in a loud voice. The others were already laughing. Ralph pushed off from the car and crossed the street. In a few minutes he came to Blake's, where he stopped some afternoons for a beer with Dick Koenig before picking up the children from nursery school.

It was dark inside. Candles flamed in long-necked bottles at the tables along one wall. Ralph glimpsed shadowy figures of men and women talking, their heads close together. One of the couples, near the door, stopped talking and looked up at him. A boxlike fixture in the ceiling revolved overhead, throwing out pins of light. Two men sat at the end of the bar, and a dark cutout of a man leaned over the jukebox in the corner, his hands splayed on each side of the glass. That man is going to play something, Ralph thought as if making a momentous discovery, and he stood in the center of the floor, watching the man.

"Ralph! Mr Wyman, sir!"

He looked around. It was David Parks calling to him from behind the bar. Ralph walked over, leaned heavily against the bar before sliding onto a stool.

"Should I draw one, Mr Wyman?" Parks held a glass in his hand, smiling. Ralph nodded, watched Parks fill the glass, watched Parks hold the glass at an angle under the tap, smoothly straighten the glass as it filled.

"How's it going, Mr Wyman?" Parks put his foot up on a shelf under the bar. "Who's going to win the game next week, Mr Wyman?" Ralph shook his head, brought the beer to his lips. Parks coughed faintly. "I'll buy you one, Mr Wyman. This one's on me." He put his leg down, nodded assurance, and reached under his apron into his pocket. "Here. I have it right here," Ralph said and pulled out some change, examined it in his hand. A quarter, nickel, two dimes, two pennies. He counted as if there were a code to be uncovered. He laid down the quarter and stood up, pushing the change back into his pocket. The man was still in front of the jukebox, his hands still out to its sides.

Outside, Ralph turned around, trying to decide what to do. His heart was jumping as if he'd been running. The door opened behind him and a man and woman came out. Ralph stepped out of the way and they got into a car parked at the curb and Ralph saw the woman toss her hair as she got into the car: He had never seen anything so frightening.

He walked to the end of the block, crossed the street, and walked another block before he decided to head downtown. He walked hurriedly, his hands balled into his pockets, his shoes smacking the pavement. He kept blinking his eyes and thought it incredible that this was where he lived. He shook his head. He would have liked to sit someplace for a while and think about it, but he knew he could not sit, could not think about it. He remembered a man he saw once sitting on a curb in Arcata, an old man with a growth of beard and a brown wool cap who just sat there with his arms between his legs. And then Ralph thought: Marian! Dorothea! Robert! It was impossible. He tried to imagine how all this would seem twenty years from now. But he could not imagine anything. And then he imagined snatching up a note being passed among his students and it said *Shall we have a go at it?* Then he could not think. Then he felt profoundly indifferent. Then he thought of Marian. He thought of Marian as he had seen her a little while ago, face crumpled. Then Marian on the floor, blood on her teeth: "Why did you hit me?" Then Marian reaching under her dress to unfasten her garter belt! Then Marian lifting her dress as she arched back! Then Marian ablaze, Marian crying out, *Go! Go! Go!*

He stopped. He believed he was going to vomit. He moved to the curb. He kept swallowing, looked up as a car of yelling teenagers went by and gave him a long blast on their musical horn. Yes, there was a great evil pushing at the world, he thought, and it only needed a little slipway, a little opening.

He came to Second Street, the part of town people called "Two Street". It started here at Shelton, under the streetlight where the old rooming-houses ended, and ran for four or five blocks on down to the pier, where fishing boats tied up. He had been down here once, six years ago, to a secondhand shop to finger through the dusty shelves of old books. There was a liquor store across the street, and he could see a man standing just inside the glass door, looking at a newspaper.

A bell over the door tinkled. Ralph almost wept from the sound of it. He bought some cigarettes and went out again, continuing along the street, looking in windows, some with signs taped up: a dance, the Shrine circus that had come and gone last summer, an election - *Fred C. Walters for Councilman*. One of the windows he looked through had sinks and pipe joints scattered around on a table, and this too brought tears to his eyes. He came to a Vic Tanney gym where he could see light sneaking under the curtains pulled across a big window and could hear water splashing in the pool inside and the echo of exhilarated voices calling across water. There was more light now, coming from bars and cafés on both sides of the street, and more people, groups of three or four, but now and then a man by himself or a woman in bright slacks walking rapidly. He stopped in front of a window and watched some Negroes shooting pool, smoke drifting in the light burning above the table. One of the men, chalking his cue, hat on, cigarette in his mouth, said something to another man and both men grinned, and then the first man looked intently at the balls and lowered himself over the table.

Ralph stopped in front of Jim's Oyster House. He had never been here before, had never been to any of these places before. Above the door the name was spelled out in yellow lightbulbs: JIM'S OYSTER HOUSE. Above this, fixed to an iron grill, there was a huge neon-lighted clam shell with a man's legs sticking out. The torso was hidden in the shell and the legs flashed red, on and off, up and down, so that they seemed to be kicking. Ralph lit another cigarette from the one he had and pushed the door open.

It was crowded, people bunched on the dance floor, their arms laced around each other, waiting in positions for the band to begin again. Ralph pushed his way to the bar, and once a drunken woman took hold of his coat. There were no stools and he had to stand at the end of the bar between a Coast Guardsman and a shriveled man in denims. In the mirror he could see the men in the band getting up from the table where they had been sitting. They wore white shirts and dark slacks with little red string ties around their necks. There was a fireplace with gas flames behind a stack of metal logs, and the band platform was to the side of this. One of the musicians plucked the strings of his electric guitar, said something to the others with a knowing grin. The band began to play.

Ralph raised his glass and drained it. Down the bar he could hear a woman say angrily, "Well, there's going to be trouble, that's all I've got to say." The musicians came to the end of their number and started another. One of the men, the bass player, moved to the microphone and began to sing. But Ralph could not understand the words. When the band took another break, Ralph looked around for the toilet. He could make out doors opening and closing at the far end of the bar and headed in that direction. He staggered a little and knew he was drunk now. Over one of the doors was a rack of antlers. He saw a man go in and he saw another man catch the door and come out. Inside, in line behind three other men, he found himself staring at opened thighs and vulva drawn on the wall over a pocket-comb machine. Beneath was scrawled EAT ME, and lower down someone had added *Betty M. Eats It – RA 52275*. The man ahead moved up, and Ralph took a step forward, his heart squeezed in the weight of Betty. Finally, he moved to the bowl and urinated. It was bolt of lightning cracking. He sighed, leaned forward, and let his head rest against the wall. Oh, Betty, he thought. His life had changed, he was willing to understand. Were there other men, he wondered drunkenly, who could look at one event in their lives and perceive in it the tiny makings of the catastrophe that thereafter set their lives on a different course? He stood there a while longer, and then he looked down: he had urinated on his fingers. He moved to the wash basin, ran water over his hands after deciding against the dirty bar of soap. As he was unrolling the towel, he put his face up close to the pitted mirror and looked into his eyes. A face: nothing out of the ordinary. He touched the glass, and then he moved away as a man tried to get past him to the sink.

When he came out the door, he noticed another door at the other end of the corridor. He went to it and looked through the glass panel in the door at four card players around a green felt table. It seemed to Ralph immensely still and restful inside, the silent movements of the men languorous and heavy with meaning. He leaned against the glass and watched until he felt the men watching him.

Back at the bar there was a flourish of guitars and people began whistling and clapping. A fat middle-aged woman in a white evening dress was being helped onto the platform. She kept trying to pull back but Ralph could see that it was mock effort, and finally she accepted the mike and made a little curtsy. The people whistled and stamped their feet. Suddenly he knew that nothing could save him but to be in the same room with the card players, watching. He took out his wallet, keeping his hands up over the sides as he looked to see how much he had. Behind him the woman began to sing in a low drowsy voice.

The man dealing looked up.

"Decided to join us?" he said, sweeping Ralph with his eyes and checking the table again. The others raised their eyes for an instant and then looked back at the cards skimming around the table. The men picked up their cards, and the man sitting with his back to Ralph breathed impressively out his nose, turned around in his chair and glared.

"Benny, bring another chair!" the dealer called to an old man sweeping under a table that had chairs turned up on the top. The dealer was a large man; he wore a white shirt, open at the collar, the sleeves rolled back once to expose forearms thick with black curling hair. Ralph drew a long breath.

"Want anything to drink?" Benny asked, carrying a chair to the table.

Ralph gave the old man a dollar and pulled out of his coat. The old man took the coat and hung it up by the door as he went out. Two of the men moved their chairs and Ralph sat down across from the dealer.

"How's it going?" the dealer said to Ralph, not looking up.

"All right," Ralph said.

The dealer said gently, still not looking up, "Low ball or five card. Table stakes, five-dollar limit on raises."

Ralph nodded, and when the hand was finished he bought fifteen dollars' worth of chips. He watched the cards as they flashed around the table, picked up his as he had seen his father do, sliding one card under the corner of another as each card fell in front of him. He raised his eyes once and looked at the faces of the others. He wondered if it had ever happened to any of them.

In half an hour he had won two hands, and, without counting the small pile of chips in front of him, he thought he must still have fifteen or even twenty dollars. He paid for another drink with a chip and was suddenly aware that he had come a long way that evening, a long way in his life. *Jackson*, he thought. He could be Jackson.

"You in or out?" one man asked. "Clyde, what's the bid, for Christ's sake?" the man said to the dealer.

"Three dollars," the dealer said.

"In," Ralph said. "I'm in." He put three chips into the pot.

The dealer looked up and then back at his cards. "You really want some action, we can go to my place when we finish here," the dealer said.

"No, that's all right," Ralph said, "Enough action tonight. I just found out tonight. My wife played around with another guy two years ago. I found out tonight." He cleared his throat.

One man laid down his cards and lit his cigar. He stared at Ralph as he puffed, then shook out the match and picked up his cards again. The dealer looked up, resting his open hands on the table, the black hair very crisp on his dark hands.

"You work here in town?" he said to Ralph.

"I live here," Ralph said. He felt drained, splendidly empty.

"We playing or not?" a man said. "Clyde?"

"Hold your water," the dealer said.

"For Christ's sake," the man said quietly.

"What did you find out tonight?" the dealer said.

"My wife," Ralph said. "I found out."

In the alley, he took out his wallet again, let his fingers number the bills he had left: two dollars – and he thought there was some change in his pocket. Enough for something to eat. But he was not hungry, and he sagged against the building trying to think. A car turned into the alley, stopped, backed out again. He started walking. He went the way he'd come. He stayed close to the buildings, out of the path of the loud groups of men and women streaming up and down the sidewalk. He heard a woman in a long coat say to the man she was with, "It isn't that way at all, Bruce. You don't understand."

He stopped when he came to the liquor store. Inside he moved up to the counter and studied the long orderly rows of bottles. He bought a half pint of rum and some more cigarettes. The palm trees on the label of the bottle, the large drooping fronds with the lagoon in the background, had caught his eye, and then he realized *rum!* And he thought he would faint. The clerk, a thin bald man wearing suspenders, put the bottle in a paper sack and rang up the sale and winked. "Got you a little something tonight?" he said.

Outside, Ralph started toward the pier; he thought he'd like to see the water with the lights reflected on it. He thought how Dr Maxwell would handle a thing like this, and he reached into the sack as he walked, broke the seal on the little bottle and stopped in a doorway to take a long drink and thought Dr Maxwell would sit handsomely at the water's edge. He crossed some old streetcar tracks and turned onto another, darker street. He could already hear the waves splashing under the pier, and then he heard someone move up behind him. A small Negro in a leather jacket stepped out in front of him and said, "Just a minute there, man." Ralph tried to move around. The man said, "Christ, baby, that's my feet you're steppin' on!" Before Ralph could run the Negro hit him hard in the stomach, and when Ralph groaned and tried to fall, the man hit him in the nose with his open hand, knocking him back against the wall, where he sat down with one leg turned under him and was learning how to raise himself up when the Negro slapped him on the cheek and knocked him sprawling onto the pavement.

III

He kept his eyes fixed in one place and saw them, dozens of them, wheeling and darting just under the overcast, seabirds, birds that came in off the ocean this time of morning. The street was black with the mist that was still falling, and he had to be careful not to step on the snails that trailed across the wet sidewalk. A car with its lights on slowed as it went past. Another car passed. Then another. He looked: mill workers, he whispered to himself. It was Monday morning. He turned a corner, walked past Blake's: blinds pulled, empty bottles standing like sentinels beside the door. It was cold. He walked as fast as he could, crossing his arms now and then and rubbing his shoulders. He came at last to his house, porch light on, windows dark. He crossed the lawn and went around to the back. He turned the knob, and the door opened quietly and the house was quiet. There was the tall stool beside the draining board. There was the table where they had sat. He had gotten up from the couch, come into the kitchen, sat down. What more had he done? He had done nothing more. He looked at the clock over the stove. He could see into the dining room, the table with the lace cloth, the heavy glass centerpiece of red flamingos, their wings opened, the draperies beyond the table open. Had she stood at that window watching for him? He stepped onto the living-room carpet. Her coat was thrown over the couch, and in the pale light he could make out a large ashtray full of her cork cigarette ends. He noticed the phone directory open on the coffee table as he went by. He stopped at the partially open door to their bedroom. Everything seemed to him open. For an instant he resisted the wish to look in at her, and then with his finger he pushed the door open a little bit more. She was sleeping, her head off the pillow, turned toward the wall, her hair black against the sheet, the covers bunched around her shoulders, covers pulled up from the foot of the bed. She was on her side, her secret body angled at the hips. He stared. What, after all, should he do? Take his things and leave? Go to a hotel? Make certain arrangements? How should a man act, given these circumstances? He understood things had been done. He did not understand what things now were to be done. The house was very quiet.

In the kitchen he let his head down onto his arms as he sat at the table. He did not know what to do. Not just now, he thought, not just in this, not just about this, today and tomorrow, but every day on earth. Then he heard the children stirring. He sat up and tried to smile as they came into the kitchen.

"Daddy, Daddy," they said, running to him with their little bodies.

"Tell us a story, Daddy," his son said, getting onto his lap.

"He can't tell us a story," his daughter said. "It's too early for a story. Isn't it, Daddy?"

"What's that on your face, Daddy?" his son said, pointing.

"Let me see!" his daughter said. "Let me see, Daddy."

"Poor Daddy," his son said.

"What did you do to your face, Daddy?" his daughter said.

"It's nothing," Ralph said. "It's all right, sweetheart. Now get down now, Robert, I hear your mother."

Ralph stepped quickly into the bathroom and locked the door.

"Is your father here?" he heard Marian calling. "Where is he, in the bathroom? Ralph?"

"Mama, Mama!" his daughter cried. "Daddy's face is hurt!"

"Ralph!" She turned the knob. "Ralph, let me in, please, darling. Ralph? Please let me in, darling. I want to see you. Ralph? Please!"

He said, "Go away, Marian."

She said, "I can't go away. Please, Ralph, open the door for a minute, darling. I just want to see you. Ralph. Ralph? The children said you were hurt. What's wrong, darling? Ralph?"

He said, "Go away."

She said, "Ralph, open up, please."

He said, "Will you please be quiet, please?"

He heard her waiting at the door, he saw the knob turn again, and then he could hear her moving around the kitchen, getting the children breakfast, trying to answer their questions. He looked at himself in the mirror a long time. He made faces at himself. He tried many expressions. Then he gave it up. He turned away from the mirror and sat down on the edge of the bathtub, began unlacing his shoes. He sat there with a shoe in his hand and looked at the clipper ships making their way across the wide blue sea of the plastic shower curtain. He thought of the little black coaches in the tablecloth and almost cried out *Stop!* He unbuttoned his shirt, leaned over the bathtub with a sigh, and pressed the plug into the drain. He ran hot water, and presently steam rose.

He stood naked on the tiles before getting into the water. He gathered in his fingers the slack flesh over his ribs. He studied his face again in the clouded mirror. He started in fear when Marian called his name.

"Ralph. The children are in their room playing. I called Von Williams and said you wouldn't be in today, and I'm going to stay home." Then she said, "I have a nice breakfast on the stove for you, darling, when you're through with your bath. Ralph?"

"Just be quiet, please," he said.

He stayed in the bathroom until he heard her in the children's room. She was dressing them, asking didn't they want to play with Warren and Roy? He went through the house and into the bedroom, where he shut the door. He looked at the bed before he crawled in. He lay on his back and stared at the ceiling. He had gotten up from the couch, had come into the kitchen, had . . . *sat* . . . *down.* He snapped shut his eyes and turned onto his side as Marian came into the room. She took off her robe and sat down on the bed. She put her hand under the covers and began stroking the lower part of his back.

"Ralph," she said.

He tensed at her fingers, and then he let go a little. It was easier to let go a little. Her hand moved over his hip and over his stomach and she was pressing her body over his now and moving over him and back and forth over him. He held himself, he later considered, as long as he could. And then he turned to her. He turned and turned in what might have been a stupendous sleep, and he was still turning, marveling at the impossible changes he felt moving over him.

BY RAYMON CARVER
ALSO AVAILABLE FROM VINTAGE